OUT
GAMED

LILA ROSE
USA TODAY BESTSELLING AUTHOR

Out Gamed Copyright © 2019 by Lila Rose

Cover Design: Letitia Hasser
Cover Photograph: Wander Aguiar
Editing: Hot Tree Editing
Interior Design: Rogena Mitchell-Jones

Out Gamed is a work of fiction. All names, characters, events and places found in this book are either from the author's imagination or used fictitiously. Any similarity to persons live or dead, actual events, locations, or organizations is entirely coincidental and not intended by the author.

First Edition

CHAPTER ONE

NANCY

*T*hroughout my fifty-five years, I'd experienced a lot. Some moments had been so great I couldn't have been happier than at those times, because I'd been surrounded by a lot of love. My children were my life. If they weren't happy or content, I couldn't settle until they were. I didn't realise how much of my love, my life, or my happiness also depended on Richard.

When I lost him, a whole chunk of myself ripped free from my body and died along with him. My heart and soul would never be the same. *Ever.* He was the man of my dreams, the man I couldn't see my life without, and yet, there I was, in the world without him. After three years of losing him, somehow, I still survived.

Only I did it each day with pain in my existence.

No one, not my daughters, son, or sons-in-law, knew I'd wished for death. I'd prayed for it because I didn't think I could live on without him. I'd yearned for death every waking moment for a long time hoping to see his face, hear his voice, or touch his warm skin once more.

Only God had another wish for me. There must have been some reason he wanted me to stick around. I just didn't know for sure what it was. It could possibly be for my grandchildren. I also realised, though, ending my life would have been selfish. It would have hurt so many I would never want to upset in any way.

So, with my grandkids as my only focus, they became a new light in my life.

Ones that lifted me up and kept me going after I'd been weak, hurting, and suffering. I hadn't been able to stop crying unless they were around. I hadn't been able to stop aching and feeling hollow unless they were there.

Though I'd been better in the last year, I couldn't stop the dull ache of not having my Richard with me. He was the man I'd love for the rest of my life. So, while we celebrated birthdays, weddings, and every special occasion, I'd keep loving him each and every day.

Not letting anyone take his place.

I'd endure each passing day without him in it and cherish the dreams I shared with him most nights.

It was the other nights I didn't care for.

The nights that had me waking and feeling so empty.

Those nights were the ones where I dreamed of losing Richard over again.

While I stood surrounded by friends and family, I couldn't help but think of the dream from the previous night.

As I sat on the couch, I looked over at my handsome husband, who a lot of the times drove me crazy, but I still loved him. I winked at him when he glanced my way before asking, "Are you ready for bed, honey?"

"Always ready when you ask like that." He grinned. Even though I knew we wouldn't be making love that night since Richard hadn't

been feeling well all day, I still liked to go to bed with him at my side, and he knew it. I grabbed the remote, turned off the TV, and stood from the couch. Richard groaned as he straightened from his chair. He took my hand as I went to pass, and stopped me, turning me into him. I wrapped my arms around his waist and smiled up at him as his palms slid up my arms to my shoulders.

"Have I told you lately how damn lucky I am to have you in my life? To have you agree to be my wife and have our kids? Even when I'm ready to throttle you a lot of the time, I wouldn't change anything in our lives."

My eyes warmed as I teased, "I can't exactly remember me agreeing to be your wife, more the fact you had got me knocked up with Zara."

"It was my plan all along."

I laughed. "Sure it was." When I was nineteen and found out I was pregnant, it had been a shock, especially since Richard and I hadn't been dating long, but he was right. I wouldn't change any of it. Sobering, I said, "What's brought all this on?"

He shrugged. "I was thinking about us and how gifted we've been in our lives. I don't think I tell you enough I love you."

I smiled softly. "You tell me nearly every day, but I can always use more." Reaching up, I pressed my lips against his. "Love you forever and always, my Richie Rich."

"Of course you will. You'll—" His hands dropped to his chest, his eyes widening. "Nance," he groaned.

Shards of my heart broke off and swept throughout my body, slicing me over and over. I gripped his arms and cried, "No, Richard, no!" Being a nurse, I knew the signs. My experience kicked in, and somehow through my fear, I managed to get him sitting, check his vitals, and call an ambulance. In that time, Richard had not one, but two heart attacks.

Panic sliced through me, threatening to take me to the ground and *give up. But I couldn't. He needed me. He had to be okay. The thought of him not surviving this.... It killed me to even think that.*

In the ambulance on the way to the hospital, I rang Zara and Mattie. They were going to get to the hospital as soon as they could, and also call our foster daughter, Josie, in Melbourne. Somehow, I managed to keep it together through the calls, but when I hung up and looked down at Richard, my eyes welled. Despite the oxygen mask, his breathing was still shallow. Fear spiked in my veins and clawed at my chest. I shook my head again and again. This can't be happening. His hand came out towards me, and I took it as a sob caught in my throat. Bending, I tightened both hands around his one, and rested my head on his shoulder.

"Don't leave me," I begged, my voice catching. "Please, don't leave me."

"Love you, Nance," I heard whispered behind his mask.

I shook my head against his shoulder. "Don't," I pleaded. "Don't," I cried.

"Nance, love you always and forever."

"Always and forever," I murmured into his ear, my voice clogged with emotions while my stomach churned in turmoil.

Within moments of arriving, he was rushed into testing, but the news wasn't good. They gave him until morning.

Morning.

How was I supposed to deal with news like that?

I couldn't. I didn't want to, but I had to. For Richard and for our children.

A hand on my arm dragged me from my thoughts. "Nancy, are you all right?"

I smiled shakily at Ivy. She was a good friend to my daughter Zara. I knew she noticed my smile wasn't fully there when her brows pinched.

I kept at it and reached for her hand. I nodded. "I'm fine." It was then I noticed deep sea-blue eyes staring at me. It was one of the Hawks brothers—the club my son-in-law Talon was president of—leaning against the door frame at the entrance of the hall to the living room of Easton's home. Shock at his attention had my lips thinning. Then I snorted to myself and glanced behind me to see where his attention really sat. No one stood there. Worried, I nibbled my bottom lip. Perhaps I had something on my face, but surely Ivy would have pointed it out.

When the front door opened to Easton's house, it drew my attention away from the biker with the intense stare and nice, but naughty half smile.

Ivy sucked in a sharp breath. "Oh my," she muttered.

Oh my, indeed. Easton was damn hot. It was the first time we'd set eyes on the man. We'd arrived en masse to meet him for the first time because he was a part of Lan's life—Lan being a friend to us all and the Hawks MC.

I heard the back door open and saw Lan there, his eyes only for Easton. He walked right up to him, since Easton looked about ready to run. Not that I could blame him; there were a lot of us there to meet him. Lan leaned in and kissed him, the move natural and sweet. When they whispered to each other, I smiled broadly; they looked wonderful together.

Honestly, I couldn't have been prouder of the people around me. Since Talon had claimed Zara as his woman, then his wife, our lives had become richer with so many amazing people. The men in Talon's club were rough and gruff, but they all had big hearts, and it showed by the way they supported one another.

"Come on," Deanna, Zara's best friend, called. "Enough monopolising his time. You can have him later."

Lan ignored her for a moment more and muttered something to Easton, who grinned and replied with a chuckle, "I'll be fine."

"All right," we all heard Lan say before he nodded and turned to stand beside his guy. "Everyone, this is Easton. Easton, everyone... who I'm sure will introduce themselves. Don't scare him off. I want him to stay long-term."

"OMG, that is the cutest thing to say ever," my son-in-law Julian cooed. People laughed, and I was one of them. Julian was a beautiful, extraordinary man, and I couldn't have been happier when our son, Matthew, told us he was in love with Julian. I knew it would stick and they'd last the distance, and they had. Now married, they also had their own daughter, my grandbaby Aelia, thanks to the help from Zara.

Lan took the ice from Easton's friend Oliver, who we'd met earlier, then kissed Easton one last time before he headed for the back door.

"Hey." Zara smiled. "I know you won't remember *all* of our names, but I'd like to try and introduce you to those around here."

Easton smiled warmly and nodded. "I'd like that."

"Great. I'm Zara. Talon is outside with all the guys. He's the president of all Hawks chapters. I'll introduce you to him later. My tribe consists of Cody, who's outside with the men, Maya, Drake, and Ruby." She pointed to my grandchildren, all of them good—sometimes cheeky—but sweet and thoughtful kids. "Next to me is Deanna. Her two are Swan and Nicholas. That's Ivy, who's a couple of months pregnant. Same as Mally, who I've been told you already know." Easton nodded and waved at the already smiling and waving Mally, Lan's cousin's wife. Zara went on, "Clary, with her bundle of joy playing on the floor is Logan. My mum, Nancy."

Not being able to help myself, I stepped up and said,

"You're damn handsome, young man. Are you sure you bat for the other team?"

Easton snorted through a laugh. "Yes."

"I don't," was called out. I, along with everyone else, turned to the only biker guy left in the room. He still stood leaning, with his huge arms crossed, against the hallway door frame. His voice was deep, yet playful.

Confused, I dropped my brows and asked, "Don't what?"

"Bat for the other team." He winked, and I tensed. "Just thought you should know."

My cheeks blazed with heat. Why would *he* think *I* would want to know that? The room fell silent. Not even the children made a peep.

He couldn't be... *flirting* with me, could he? That would be ridiculous and annoying and... I didn't know right then, but I felt peeved by it. I glared over at him and told him some truths. "I'm old enough to be your mother. It's okay for me to mess about, but it's another story for young men to play people."

He smirked his full lips, shook his head of dark buzzed-cut hair, and straightened. "Darlin', I ain't messin', and age is just a number." With that, he walked out of the room, and I followed him with my eyes, shocked by his words.

"Age is just a number." Pfft, please.

He "ain't messing." Yes, sure I believe that.

"Nancy, I think he was just coming onto you," Julian said, sounding serious.

I scoffed, still glaring in the man's direction. Finally, I said, "Don't be stupid, Julian."

"He's not, Nance," Deanna offered; she also sounded serious.

I shook my head and turned back to everyone. "It doesn't

matter if he was or wasn't. Richard was the love of my life, and no one could replace him."

"Doesn't mean you can't be happy," Zara said quietly.

I studied my daughter. My eyes softened knowing my girl wanted me happy. "I am happy, baby," I told her, smiling. Knowing it wasn't a full one, I hid behind humour and added, "Besides, I have the super-powered vibrator Julian got me."

"You got my mother a vibrator?" Mattie, my son, bellowed. He held his little girl in his arms. She looked up at him and giggled, slapping him in the cheek.

"Now, poppet," Julian cooed. "I love you, but our mumma bear has got to have some—"

Dear God.

"Julian! Mattie!" I cried and threw my hands in the air when I glanced out back and saw men looking in from the outbursts. "Great," I snapped. "Let's share that with everyone in the world, my sons."

Mattie held his free hand to his stomach, as if he felt ill talking about my pleasure. It was kind of funny. "This is why I stay outside," he said as he handed Aeila off to Julian, and stomped his way out the back.

"Mum, what's a vibrator?" Maya, Zara's eldest daughter, asked. A moment later, Maya's lips twitched. The cheeky girl was messing with her mother. It was perfect. I turned to hide my smile and rearrange my expression before I spun back.

"Yeah, Low. I want to know, too," Rommy asked. Rommy and her brother Texas were Dodge's niece and nephew. Not that they got treated that way. After their mother had died, Dodge took them in, even when Low and Dodge's relationship had been so new, and now they brought the kids up as if they were their own.

Hawks men were big-hearted saviours.

Except for the one who'd just left.

He looked shifty because, seriously, why would he say that to me in the first place?

Low stepped back and looked to the door for an exit, wanting to be anywhere else rather than answering that question. Thankfully, she thought of a way out and said, "Romania, come back to me when you're eighteen and ask again. *Then* I'll answer."

Rommy seemed to think it over and then nodded with a smile. "Okay." She went back to building Lego with Swan, Drake, and Ruby.

As Mally, her daughter Nary, and Low drifted over to Easton, Zara, Deanna, Julian, and Ivy got close to me. I knew what was coming. I just wasn't sure if I could be bothered listening to it.

"Mum—"

"Honey, I know what you're going to say, and I promise I'm happy. I don't need some man... guy... boy to keep me happy. I love my life the way it is." The lie felt bitter. Yet it wasn't really a lie, only a partial lie. I did love my life, my children, my grandkids, but I was lonely. I missed Richard.

How could I completely love my life without him in it?

"Gamer's a nice guy," Julian tried.

I rolled my eyes. "Gamer? What type of name is that? A pubescent teen name, that's what it is." Though admittedly, his body was all man. It had been impossible not to notice. Still... "He probably lives his life playing video games like *Space Invaders* or something. Spending all his nights up late, and then sleeping all day. He wouldn't get anything done like a real man should."

They all stared at me.

Ivy cleared her throat. "Well, he likes computer games, but

I'm sure he doesn't play them all the time. I heard he got his name because he can fix or do anything with a computer, as if it's all just a game for him. He's really smart. And hell, he's really good-looking."

I took Ivy's hand in mine. "You're a sweetheart." I then glanced to them all. "You all are for worrying about me and my happiness, but I don't need your worry. I'm fine. I'm happy." I ensured my smile appeared more relaxed and genuine. "Let's get out there and enjoy the barbeque."

They relented and started to gather the kids to take them outside. Only I should have predicted Julian would take hold of my wrist and hold me back for a moment so he could whisper, "I'm sure no vibrator could make a woman feel special or look at them like he was looking at you."

Smiling at his ridiculousness, and ignoring the extra beat in my chest when I remembered Gamer's intense eyes, I asked, "How do you *think* he was looking at me?"

"Like he wanted to take you for a test run between the sheets."

Shaking off his hold, I patted his arm, trapped between amusement and emotion that caught in my chest. "But the thing about vibrators is that they don't talk back." *Or die.*

He started to smile, but it dropped away. His eyes gentled when he said, "Nor can you get hurt by them."

"Julian—"

He leaned in and kissed my cheek. Once close, he whispered, "I know, mumma bear. That hurt never goes away, but it's about learning to live with it and still get what you want."

When he shifted back, I shook my head, not wanting to talk about it or anything about my life right then. While they were only trying to reassure me, I still ached too much from losing Richard. Something they could probably see, but still, I tried again with, "When are you all going to believe me when I say I'm fine with how my life is?"

He shrugged, smiled, and then walked off, leaving me exasperated.

My kids, even if not by blood, knew me too well. Sometimes it was good, like they would know what I'd want for a gift without me hinting at it too much. Other times, like the ones where I tried to guard my emotions from them, it was frustrating. It meant I couldn't hide things from them.

Maybe one day that would change... that I'd no longer need to conceal the depth of my feelings, and perhaps eventually, I would be content in life without Richard. All I had to do was wait for that day to come and then finally, my kids would trust what I said.

I just had no idea if that day would ever truly arrive.

CHAPTER TWO

GAMER

*T*here were moments in life when a person knew they wanted something or some*one* and would do anything to get it, so certain it was just supposed to be.

One of those moments was when I minded Easton's dogs for him when he was away dealing with family issues. Those dogs were now classed as mine. In the time we'd spent together, we'd bonded. Besides, they were too goddamn cute to ignore how they'd seeped into my heart.

Another of those certain times was even more present. Certainty slammed into me when I spotted Nancy in the living room. I'd heard about her and her humour on so many occasions, long before I'd met her... well, if you could call staring from a distance meeting. Not only did she look like her daughter, Zara, a lot, only Nancy was sexier, but I'd also seen her, heard her, and smiled at the thought of having her as mine over the years. Only, I hadn't done anything about it as I knew she hadn't been ready.

When my eyes landed on her at Easton's as I came down

the hall, she was staring off in her own little world. A troubled world, I quickly realised, and something tugged at my chest. Sad thoughts seemed on her mind, making her frown and looking pained. I didn't like seeing it. I wanted to go to her and make her smile, laugh, or just take notice of me. It was likely she was thinking about her deceased husband. When Ivy caught her attention, a switch appeared to flip and she came back to herself.

My heart stuttered at the change, but I could still tell the sadness lurked. I had no idea if anyone else saw it though. She was a woman who was happy being around people she cared about.

Her smile crushed then moulded my heart into a rhythm just for her. Sounded fucking stupid, but her smile had the power to brighten a whole room.

When she spoke teasingly to Easton, her voice was raspy. It called to me, urged me to react, to draw her eyes my way. I piped up with, "I don't." When everyone in the damn roomed turned to me, I wished I'd kept my bloody mouth shut.

Confusion passed over Nancy. "Don't what?"

Fuck. I couldn't back down since she was talking to me. "Bat for the other team." I threw in a wink and felt like a douche for it. "Just thought you should know." *Jesus, shut the fuck up, man.* I caught Zara's eyes widen at my obvious attempt to flirt with her mum in front of everyone. She seemed surprised, but her small grin told me she thought it okay, and hell, that gave me hope.

Nancy's glare took me off guard. But when her words about her age followed, understanding filtered through me. She thought I was messing with her. I smirked, shook my head, and then straightened from leaning against the door frame.

"Darlin', I ain't messin', and age is just a number." With that, I walked from the room, kicking myself for even saying anything in the first place. Especially in front of everyone. But, I wanted her to notice me. Notice my attraction towards her.

For the rest of the time at Easton's, I steered clear, but she caught me looking at her a couple of times. Each moment her brows would dip. Even though I hated the thought of making her uncomfortable from my stare, I couldn't help looking. She drew me in—her voice, her actions, her whole self.

She loved big. Anyone could see it. She was sweet, funny, charming, and cheeky as well. She could talk the talk, but when it came down to it, she'd balk like she had with me. With this in mind, I kept my distance. The last thing I wanted was to scare her or make her feel trapped. I just wanted her to think about me in some way. Jesus, I felt like a teenager again with his first crush. Thank fuck none of the brothers knew about my wishing Nancy was mine or they'd either kick my arse or give me shit about it.

Considering it best if I headed out, I left the barbeque early. I had some bookwork to catch up on at the compound. I was sure I felt eyes watching me leave, but I didn't look. I hoped it was Nancy checking out my arse, and didn't want to ruin that illusion.

It was lucky I'd ridden to Easton's because, even on the bike, I struggled to get it out of the front yard since it was packed so the women could meet Easton, Lan's bed dude. He was a cool guy, easy to talk to. So was Lan though.

Once at the compound, I made my way in. The place was deserted. Almost everyone was either working or at the barbeque still. Meant I'd get more work done in peace without the brothers coming in asking for favours. Like to find someone or check someone's background or make a fake ID, or anything else they needed. It seemed my workload got bigger every damn day. I did have help with Jase, Blue's brother. He wasn't the full two-bob, but he was a great guy and smart, so fucking smart. I was teaching him the ropes on a few things, mainly the business side of all the computer work, and he flew through learning it, so at least some of it was off my back. Though, he'd been off on a trip with his misses for the last month and wasn't due back for another month.

Dodge, Blue, Memphis, and Jenny had been going out of their minds with worry about him leaving in the first place, but I knew he'd be safe in any situation, especially as he had his girl with him. Plus, the guy was older than how they still saw him. It just took time for people to know it. No matter how he was, it'd be good to have him back assisting me. Then I wouldn't have to work into the night.

A couple of hours later, I rubbed at my tired eyes. It was no good, I needed a coffee, or ten, if I was going to keep at it. Hawks had too many damned businesses to go over, and I couldn't wait until Jase was back so he could help.

Walking out of the office, I made my way down the hall. Already, the scent of freshly brewed coffee touched my senses. As soon as I stepped through the doorway to the kitchen, I stopped dead.

The only other person in the room paused too. Their eyes flashed before resuming the sip of their coffee.

Smiling, I strode over to the coffee machine, grabbed a clean mug from beside it, and poured myself a cup while thinking how fucking lucky I was. I turned and rested against the counter, sipping my own drink.

Eyes narrowed my way, my smile grew.

"Are you going to say anything?" Nancy snapped.

"What'd you like me to say?" I asked.

She shrugged. "I don't know, anything."

"I didn't get to tell you before, but you look great today."

She thinned her lips. "Anything but things like that."

"Why?"

"Because."

I waited for more, but she didn't say anything else. Instead, her attention went to the contents of her cup.

"Do I make you uncomfortable?" I asked. I didn't want that.

"Yes. No. I don't know. The things you said... back at... you know... just, don't say things like that, nor what you said a few seconds ago."

"Why?"

She shook her head. "It's not right."

"Why?"

"Jesus, Gamer, is that the only word you know?"

"No." I smirked, sipped my coffee, then added, "And call me Roman."

Her body stilled as her eyes travelled to my face. "Why?"

I raised a brow at her. Immediately, we both laughed at her mirroring my constant use of *why*. I liked it, this, us talking, laughing, and watching each other. What I didn't like was how she kept looking away from me. I wanted her warm brown eyes on me, her slim, yet curvy, short, but damn fit body facing my way. *All* of her attention turned my way, all over me. Her long dark hair, with a touch of grey, falling down around me as she rode.... Fuck. I had to stop thinking altogether or I'd embarrass myself.

I cleared my throat. "How was the rest of the barbeque?"

With the small jolt of her body, she seemed surprised by my change in conversation, but I wanted her comfortable with me.

"Ah, good. Quiet. Though Ruby and Drake do like to look for trouble all the time." She smiled fondly, staring off at the wall beside my head.

"Do you have a favourite?"

Her eyes flashed to me. "Grandchild?"

I nodded, a smirk fitted to my lips.

She scoffed. "No, I love them all the same, like my kids."

"You like being in Ballarat?"

Her brows dipped. "Yes," she drew out. "Why?"

I shrugged and moved on to another topic. "Heard Zara say before you're the best cook there is. Do you have a favourite meal you like to make?"

"Desserts, any type. Richard used to—" She froze and glanced from me to the wall. "Just dessert."

Fuck. Had I stuffed up? Did she feel she couldn't talk freely with me, even if it was about a man she loved or still did?

In a quieter tone, I asked, "What was his favourite?"

Her lips thinned and she shook her head. "Why do you want to know?"

I went for the truth. "He's a big part of your life. Knowing things about him will tell me stuff about you. I'd never want you to shy away from talking about the man who loved you, who cared for you, who gave you the kids you have, the family. Even though I didn't know him, I'd still like to know about the man who captured your heart."

Her chest rose and fell rapidly. I wasn't sure if that was good or bad. She blinked a few times before sucking in a deep breath and looking my way.

"He liked tiramisu. If he could have it every night, he would have." She studied me for a moment. "You confuse me."

I nodded. "I've been known to do that to people." Then I

smiled. I didn't miss the twitch to her sexy mouth. "For me, I've always had a thing for candy apples."

She snorted, rolled her eyes, and said, "A lot of *boys* do."

"Darlin', I ain't no boy. I'm all man."

Her pulse jumped in her neck. "So...." She looked away, but not before her eyes did a quick scan of my body. I wanted to yell in elation. Yeah, she just checked me out. If I were a peacock, I'd be preening in front of her. Light pink spread across her cheeks; she seemed flustered by the fact she'd given me a once-over. I had to get her to relax again. "What're you doin' in the compound this late anyway?"

"Talon and Zara are talking with Dodge. I'm waiting for them since they drove me here. The grandkids went home with Grady and Deanna a while ago." She bit her bottom lip. "How come you're here so late?"

"Bookwork."

"Not video games?"

I chuckled. "Only on Wednesdays." I winked.

"So no...." She shook her head and her cheeks pinked even darker. I had to know why.

"No what?"

"Nothing." She shifted, her arms crossing her chest. "I better go"

"Come on, Nancy. I thought we were gettin' along. Finish what you were gonna say."

She shook her head again, but then said, "It's stupid. I need to go find Zara." She started for the door, but I got there first, stepping in her way. Her eyes widened as her hand fluttered up to her neck and gripped the soft skin there. "Roman," she whispered.

I closed my eyes and let her voice rolling my name reach me deep. Yeah, I fucking liked hearing it. I stepped closer, hearing her gasp when my hands slid to her waist. "What were you gonna say, pumpkinhead?"

Her head jerked back, her eyes lit, her mouth opened, and she laughed hard.

Just what I wanted to hear.

"You idiot. Pumpkinhead? Seriously?"

Grinning down at her, I asked, "What? Don't like it? What about doll face?"

She shook her head still laughing and slapped my chest. "Worse."

"Pickle nose?"

She snorted through her laugh. "No!"

I didn't want to, but I knew I had to. Even when all I wanted to do was wrap her tight and kiss the hell out of her. However, I moved back and threw my hands up in the air. "Fine, none of those. But I'll find one."

She was still smiling. "If that's your suggestions so far, I say you need to give up."

"Hell no, I'll find the perfect pet name for you."

Her head twitched to the side, all mirth left.

Fuck.

I'd messed up once more.

"What in the fuck is goin' on in here?"

Turning, I stepped in front of Nancy to protect her, only I knew right away she wouldn't be the one needing protection.

Shit, maybe the lightness to the moment hadn't dropped away from Nancy because of me. It could have been from the male fuming in front of us.

"Ah, hey, boss," I offered.

Talon crossed his arms over his chest and glared. Zara peeked over his shoulder and waved. She didn't seem worried I was alone with her mum in the kitchen.

"Wanna tell me what's goin' on?" Talon asked.

Nancy sighed behind me. "We were talking, Talon. I don't think there's anything wrong with that. I talk to your guys all the time, and you don't get your jocks in a bunch."

His jaw clenched before he snarled, "That's because my *guys* don't look at you like they wanna take a chunk outta you."

"Honey—" Zara tried.

"Talon," Nancy snapped over her daughter. She stepped around me and pushed her son-in-law back with her hands on his chest. "We are not doing this."

"Would it be the wrong time to ask for Nancy's number?" I called out.

Nancy looked over her shoulder in shock. Talon sneered, gripped Nancy's shoulders and shifted her sideways, then started for me. Zara curled both her arms around her husband's waist and yelled, "Talon, no hurting him."

"I'll do more than fuckin' hurt."

My hands came up. "Boss—"

"That's fuckin' right," he snarled. "Remember your place or I can cut you fuckin' lose and you'll never—"

"Talon Marcus," Zara snapped. "You're being over the top."

Talon pointed at me. "You and I are gonna have words where there won't be women stoppin' what's to come."

I nodded. If I wanted anything with Nancy, I knew it'd take time and be a hell of a fight to prove myself to Nancy and her family.

"You're both being stupid," Nancy clipped. She stomped to stand between Talon and me. "There's nothing going on so there won't be any arguing, fighting, or maiming anyone."

"Nancy," I said lightly. She met my stare, hers a little wary, but she gave me it anyway, wanting to know what I was about to say. That meant something, didn't it? "Don't worry about us."

"I won't, because there's nothing to worry about."

Talon looked smug. I didn't like it. I had to make my intention clear to not only him, but Nancy. My gut churned at the thought of Nancy running from the room, away from me and what I wanted for us.

"Darlin', this is happenin'."

Her eyes widened.

"It ain't happenin', fucker," Talon growled out. He took hold of Nancy's wrist and steered her towards the door, all while Zara followed with a smile on her face and with Nancy looking back at me puzzled.

"What did he mean by that?" she asked near the doorway.

"Nothin'," Talon bit out.

"I'll call you, Nancy," I said loud enough to be heard.

"You fuckin' won't," Talon yelled back from down the hall.

Footsteps approached my way again. I tensed, wondering whether I'd pushed Talon too far. Zara poked her head around and rattled off a bunch of numbers. "That's her number."

I smiled wide, fucking glad I had a good memory.

"I'm trusting you, Gamer. So don't stuff her around or I will let Talon loose."

I held back my snort, knowing Talon would have his say no matter what his wife said or did. Still, I was damn grateful for her obvious approval of me with her mum. "I won't fuck her over, Wildcat." I couldn't, not when I was looking for a forever kind of thing with Nancy.

She nodded after a moment.

"Kitten," Talon barked. She disappeared, and I heard, "What'd you say to him?"

"Nothing, honey."

"Zara?" Nancy asked. Even she sounded suspicious.

"Let's get home. I'm tired."

Was she tired of me or the situation or the late night? I didn't know, but I wanted to.

Christ, I hoped Nancy would give me a chance.

Just one.

CHAPTER THREE

NANCY

This is happening. His words rolled around in my mind on the drive home while I ignored Talon's ranting—by faking sleep—about how a brother should know better than trying to cotton on to a mother-in-law.

Roman had been serious. Even though I acted dumb, I saw it in his eyes. He'd meant what he'd said. He wanted something to happen between us. I just couldn't understand why. He was so much younger than I was. He could easily have anyone he wanted; he was sexy enough.

God, I wasn't supposed to even think about how good-looking he was.

It wasn't right.

Richard was my life.

My head was jumbled. I didn't know what to think of Roman and his straightforwardness.

I didn't want to acknowledge the way my belly dipped, the way my heart thumped when he was close, when he looked at me or smiled.

It wasn't right.

Suddenly, I felt like crying because my mind kept telling me I was spitting on Richard's grave for even reacting to Roman, for thinking of him.

"Mum," Zara called. "You're home."

Straightening, I clasped her shoulder and gave it a squeeze. "Thanks for the lift."

"Nancy—" Talon started.

"I'll talk to you both tomorrow. I'm tired." I opened the car door, got out, and closed it behind me. Once at the front door, I unlocked it, and turned and waved before I entered, knowing they wouldn't leave until I was safely inside.

I slumped back against the door. In front of me sat a picture of Richard. My chest ached. My bottom lip wobbled. "I'm sorry," I whispered.

Maybe Talon was right, that Roman shouldn't be trying with me. I didn't need or deserve his attention. Richard had been my one true love, and I was happy with that. I didn't need to find it again. I shouldn't want to.

Richard was my life.

"I'm sorry," I sobbed again. I was sorry for thinking of Roman, for reacting and looking, admiring.

"Don't be sorry, Nance. You got a lotta love in you to give."

I shook my head, trying to clear his voice from my mind. I shook it again. "Not for another man."

"Yes."

I groaned and wiped at my face. "How could I imagine that? Richard wouldn't want me with another man." *But he'd want me happy.* "No," I muttered. *He would.*

Growling under my breath, I speed-walked into my room, threw my bag on the bed, and got undressed. Sleep. I needed to rest before I went crazy. Well, crazier.

It was a few days later, where I had managed to avoid Talon and Zara by claiming I was too busy and had taken on more shifts at the hospital, when a knock came at the front door. I put the dishrag down and made my way to the door. Opening it, all I could see were flowers.

My heart twisted.

Only, I wasn't sure if it was in sadness because Richard used to give me flowers all the time or in the excitement of the nice surprise.

"Nancy Alexander," a male voice said from behind the large bouquet.

"Yes, that's me."

"Delivery," he said the obvious and thrust the flowers my way. I took them, thanked him, and closed the door. It was a little struggle because they were so heavy, but I managed to carry them into the kitchen, setting them on the table since they were already in a vase.

Stepping back, I spotted the card sticking out of the top of the arrangement. I grabbed it, ignoring how my hands shook a little as I opened it.

It read: *What about, sexy legs?*

I clamped my bottom lip down with my top teeth, and yet a smile grew over. I couldn't help it. My belly fluttered to life.

Sexy legs.

I laughed.

Roman was different.

It was like he knew I'd be… scared, worried, hurt… hell, feeling guilty, so he wanted to make me smile, laugh even.

How did he even get my address? Wait, he was a computer genius apparently; he'd have his ways of finding out.

On the kitchen counter, my phone chimed with a text. Still smiling, I went over, picked it up, and a number I didn't recognised flashed up. Before I saw the preview to the message, I opened it.

Did you like the flowers?

There went my stomach again.

I bit my nail, worried my bottom lip with my top teeth, and then sucked in a big cup of courage, along with air, while I ignored the stab of guilt in the back of my mind. **I did, thank you.**

He responded right away. **Thoughts on sexy legs?**

A giggle escaped. *Silly man.* **No!**

Damn, I thought that was a good one.

Why did you send me flowers?

Because I was thinking of you.

Dear God, that was sweet.

Why did he have to be so sweet? I could turn him away, I should, but I hadn't felt this... alive, in such a long time.

Did I lose you?

No. It was all I could reply with. Where had my wit gone? My teasing? Drained away because I knew he was being real. Roman was *interested* in me. Knowing it made my brain short circuit.

Good. How have you been?

Small talk. He wanted to do small talk, and I wasn't sure I was up for it. Also, I didn't know what I wanted.

Um, good. You?

Same boring self. Tell me something about you.

Shit. I didn't know what to tell him. I scrambled for something, anything, feeling as though I had to keep this conversation going. The knowledge made me pause as I considered why that was. Admittedly, I liked the attention.

Pain sliced through my body.

Was I just using Roman to feel something other than hollow?

Am I that mean to use him?

Am I using him?

Roman hadn't ever been on my radar until now. Since I knew he liked me, he passed through my mind a lot more than I wanted to admit to myself.

I shouldn't keep this going.

Stuff it all to hell. I was a big ball of confusion. Did it make me a bad person to want this, even if it was only texting with Roman? Did I like him? I couldn't, shouldn't, and yet, from the moment he'd flirted, he'd pulled a reaction from me. He affected me. I couldn't ignore the possibility it was only because he showed me attention, though. My stomach dipped at that.

I dropped my phone to the table and walked away from it. "What am I supposed to do?" I asked myself. Only I didn't have any answers.

My phone chimed. I gripped my neck with one hand and the sink with the other. I spun, and strode to the phone, snatching it up.

Are you okay?

How dare he ask. How dare he be nice to me when I could be using him. Holy shit, I was losing the plot. I didn't know who he was really. I simply saw his smile, his joking nature... but what was he really like, and more terrifying was, did I honestly want to know?

I don't know.

We're just texting, Nancy. Talking. No harm can come from it. If you've ever had enough of me, you tell me. Just want to get to know you. If you're okay with it.

That was the thing. I didn't know if I was okay with it, but he was right: there was no harm to texting. Right? They were just words. Learning about each other. We could become friends, and somehow, I knew he would accept whatever I wanted us to be. Friends were good to have no matter the sex or age.

Bloody hell.

Okay. We'll text. I hit Send, and my heart thumped hard in my chest. I didn't know if I was happy with my choice or not.

I have to get back to work, but I'll text you later, yeah?

I thinned my lips because my mouth wanted to smile.

Friends.

It was all I had in me. If I thought of anything more, then I could possibly be put in the loony bin.

I had to put the phone down, run my hands through my hair a few times, drag in a ragged breath and then, finally, I was able to pick up the phone and type: **Yes.**

Then I quickly added: **I think so.** I groaned right after I pressed Send.

Great, Roman probably thought I was actually crazy instead of part way there. At least it was only texting. I couldn't bugger up texting too much. If I did, I could blame my age and autocorrect. My children and grandchildren knew autocorrect had gotten the best of me on a few occasions.

When my phone rang, I gasped and clutched my neck, staring at it as if it grew feet, hair, and sprouted a face. Only when I saw Julian's name on the screen did my racing heart relax a little.

I answered, "Hello, sweetheart."

"Hey, mumma bear, just wanted to check you haven't forgotten your pampering appointment with me this afternoon."

What happened if Roman texted while Julian was here doing my nails? My cheeks heated knowing he may find out I was texting a younger man. A man around my son-in-law's age. God, Roman could even be younger.

What was I doing?

I couldn't play with Roman. It was wrong.

"Mumma bear, what's going on?"

Clearing my throat, I hummed, then answered, "Nothing."

"Nancy," Julian whined. "No lying to your favourite SOL."

"I don't have favourites." I smiled.

He scoffed. "Yeah, all right. Wink, wink. But still, no lying about what's on your mind. You can tell me anything."

Could I?

Yes, I knew I could, but I wasn't sure I was ready to confess I was conversing with a male so much younger than myself. It was harmless, but it could lead to more. Maybe. If I let it. Though, I wasn't sure I could.

God, I had to get out of my head.

"Roman."

"Who's Roman?"

I groaned. "Gamer," I whispered, like it was the biggest secret.

"Yes?" he drew out, and I just knew there was a smile in his voice.

"He's...."

"What?" Julian cried.

"He sent me flowers just now and wants to text me, get to know me. I'm worried because... because I could be using him to make myself feel good."

"How does it make you feel good?"

Lifting my hand, I pinched my bottom lip as I thought

29

about the best way to tell him what I didn't fully understand myself.

"I smile. I feel lighter on the inside. Still, I worry, Julian."

"Of course you do, mumma bear. But have a think about this. Did you get the same feelings you have now when that doctor was up in your business wanting a piece of Nancy cake?"

Smiling at his wording, I remembered how I didn't, and at the time I wondered what was wrong with me. Doctor Hendrick, who was a few years younger than me, was a good-looking man. Only I didn't—*and still don't, since he hasn't given up*—get any type of giddy feelings like what I got with Roman.

Why was Roman different?

"Well, no, but maybe he could grow on me still."

Julian hummed. "Oh, honey, if he ain't on your mind now, he never will be. Is Gamer on your mind?"

He was.

Why?

"Yes," I whispered.

"You sound guilty for even admitting it, mumma bear. You don't need to feel guilt over enjoying life, over feeling something for another man. Richard, God rest his soul, would want, above anything, you happy. If you're worried about the age difference, don't. No one will care. Heck, look at me and your son. I became his sugar daddy, and you and Rich didn't bat an eye at it. You do what you want, Nancy Alexander. It's time to shine again."

"I'm not ready to shine."

"Well then, it's time to glow at a slow, steady pace."

A laugh escaped me. My son-in-law was crazy, but in the best way. Honestly, he suited the family; we were all a little strange.

"I'll see what I can do."

"Good. Now, are we still on for the pampering this afternoon?"

"Yes, please."

"Great, now do you want me to bring the wax? I could trim up the muff—"

"Whose muff are you talking about?" I heard my son call in the background.

"Your mum's, poppet."

"Jesus, Julian. You're not going near her... area there."

"Oh relax, baby. I've been trimming up her flower for years, well, when it was seeing action—"

"Julian!" Mattie and I cried at the same time.

"I do not want to know," Mattie added.

"Why not, it's a good spot. You came out of it—"

There was some gagging.

"I'm going," I yelled through the phone. "And please stop torturing my son about my vagina."

Julian started to laugh. "But it's fun. So the wax?"

"No, my muff isn't ready for any action."

"Yet," Julian sang.

A thought of Roman, looking up at me with a cheeky smile on his lips, flashed through my mind. My belly dipped, my pulse raced, and even my hands shook. It seemed I didn't mind that thought at all... but I wasn't sure I'd ever be ready to accept someone in my bed again, no matter how my body reacted to a certain someone.

"Bye, Julian," I said, instead of saying anything else.

CHAPTER FOUR

GAMER

*a*s I sat in the compound at the bar with some brothers, I thought about dinner the previous night at Easton's. I wasn't sure why I told Lan about my past. About my father making me watch as he shot my own dogs when I was a boy because I hadn't fucking taken the rubbish out. Maybe it was because I wanted him to understand why I'd taken a shine to Easton's animals so quickly. Why I felt the need to have his mutts in my life. I couldn't seem to bring myself to stay away from them. My life had been shit. A mother who died young, a father who didn't give a fuck, unless it was when I was doing something wrong. Those reasons were why, when I was still a teen, Hawks MC called to me. It was lucky I had skills with the computer when the old president was a major dick dragging the club through illegal crap.

Thank fuck things were better.

I was more relaxed in the years since Dodge took over. I'd never shared about myself with my brothers until recently, until I felt I could trust. And even though Lan wasn't patched in, I could talk about anything with him.

Though, it could have been just about the dogs. Still, it'd been great to see them. I hadn't realised I'd missed them a load. With a silent snort, I smiled at the thought of Easton, Lan, and Parker. Lan was Easton's man... or was it the other way around? I wasn't sure, nor did I care. However, there was also something going on with Parker and those two. Didn't know if they realised it was easy to tell. When I'd walked in yesterday, Easton looked like he'd been pashing someone, and Lan had been out the back with me, so when Parker turned a corner looking guilty, I knew he'd been the one locking lips with Easton. Lan didn't seem to care his man was making out with another. It was then I caught Parker's brief touch to Lan and knew the three of them had something going on. They didn't voice it, so I kept my mouth shut.

Each to their own and all that crap.

Still, seeing them interacting had me wishing I could just pop in on Nancy and spend time in her presence. We'd been texting every damn day. It wasn't enough. I needed to see her smile, hear her laugh in person, and maybe even share my own personal thoughts with her in some way.

I knew she wasn't ready for me to go full-steam ahead, and I respected that.

Didn't mean seeing each other face-to-face would be a bad thing.

"Hey, Gamer, where you headin'?" Nurse asked when I shifted away from the bar. I'd only had one drink, making it safe for a ride to the countryside.

"For a ride," I replied with a flick of my wrist over my shoulder. Hopefully my clipped tone was enough to steer anyone away from wanting to join me, and since I only got chuckles in response, I guessed they read me right. That or they thought I was off texting Nancy. Apparently, gossip had spread after the barbeque at Easton's, and now they all give me shit for lusting for an older lady.

Something I didn't give a shit about.

When I was just near the door to the hallway, it opened. I paused, not knowing who this huge motherfucker was. He stopped in the doorway and scanned the room.

I was just about to open my mouth when, across the room, the president boomed, "Holy fuck, Jesus Christ. Warden has graced us with his presence."

A damned big grin came over Warden's face, and it changed him completely. He didn't look like he wanted to kill everyone in the room anymore. I'd heard of Warden. He worked with Violet, Talon's sister in Ballarat, at a private investigation office.

"Dodge, I heard you're runnin' this joint. Had to see it for myself."

Dodge strode forward, his hand out, and smiling just as big as Warden. "Fuck, brother. It's good to see you."

"You too." Warden nodded, taking Dodge's hand before bringing it into himself for a quick hug-pat welcome.

"Who do we have here?" Dodge asked, stepping back and to the side. Before Warden could answer though, Dive and Vicious came forward to greet Warden in the same way.

Hell, he must have been well liked in Ballarat, which made me wonder why the brothers of Caroline Springs hadn't seen the guy before.

I caught Vicious nodding to someone behind Warden. Who in the fuck was he hiding?

"Brothers," Warden started as he shifted into the room more and stepped to the side to reveal a young woman. "This is my woman, Emerson."

Shit. Guess I wasn't the only one switching things up. The

girl looked close to twenty years his junior. Then again, I could see the goddamn love shining from each of them as they looked at each other.

Warden lifted his arm and Emerson was on the move before he had it all the way up to burrow into his side. When she brought her arm up and curved around his gut, I noticed her scars.

I wasn't the only one.

"The fuck?" Vicious snarled.

Emerson caught his gaze on her arm and dropped it, even shifted it behind her back.

"It's okay, baby doll." Warden kissed the top of her head, and reached around to pull her arm back in front. "They're just like the other Hawks brothers. Protective of women."

She eyed us all quickly, then glanced up at her man and nodded.

Dodge cleared his throat. "When did, ah, you two happen?" Meaning how long had she been free of whatever hell hole she'd been in.

"Years. Why I couldn't come here in the first place to deal with security. Took me a while to win her over, but I did." He grinned at her, and she rolled her eyes, but did it smiling.

"All good, brother. I wired the system myself, and then later Gamer fixed it when it went to shit."

Warden chuckled while his woman smiled at her feet.

I stepped up, hand out. "Name's Gamer."

Warden looked me over, took my hand and smirked. "Heard about you. The women talk. Good luck with gettin' to Nance through Talon."

Snorting, I grinned. "Reckon I'll need it, but I'm determined." I caught Dodge's eyes. "I'm headin' out. Call if you need me." He gave me a chin lift. "Good to meet you both." I nodded.

"You too," Warden said, while Emerson gave me a small wave.

Since it was already late in the afternoon, I decided to head to my room first to grab a bag in case I ended up staying in Ballarat at the compound there. I wouldn't ask or expect or even want to stay at Nancy's. I just wanted to see her for a while, get my fill and head out, that's if she'd want to see my sorry arse. Hell, maybe I should call ahead. Then again, the thought of surprising her was something I liked.

Instead, I grabbed my phone out of my back pocket and dialled Wildcat—Zara—she'd know her mum's whereabouts.

"Hello?"

"Hey, Gamer here."

Silence and then hesitantly and quietly. "Gamer?"

"Who the fuck is it?" I heard in the background.

"It's just Deanna, honey. Be back, she... ah, wants to talk about her period."

"Jesus," Talon bit out.

I chuckled, happily surprised Wildcat had my back. She really was up for me and her mum it seemed.

"Gamer, everything okay?" she asked once free.

"Know I could be puttin' you on the spot, but I'm gonna risk askin' anyway. I'm headin' to Ballarat, wantin' to surprise Nancy with a visit. You think she'd be up for it?"

She made a noise in the back of her throat. "Yes," she squeaked. "I'm sure she would."

My fucking smile near cracked my face. "Fan-fuckin'-tastic. You willin' to share where she's at?" Eagerness ran through my veins at the thought of seeing Nancy.

"Usually she'd be at home by now after work, but she's gone

to a pub with some work people. I'm not sure how long she'll be there for."

"What's it called?"

As soon as she gave me the name, I thanked her and got on my way.

It was just hitting dinner time when I rocked into Ballarat. The pub wasn't hard to find, and thank fuck there was a spot right out front so I could keep an eye on my ride through the huge windows.

Walking into the dim-lit place, I got a few concerned gazes when they glanced at my cut. Little did they know I wasn't there to cause trouble. Instead, my whole focus was to gaze at my future woman.

Christ, that made me sound like a stalker or a fucking weirdo.

Shit, my gut picked that moment to eat itself in goddamn nerves.

What happened if she didn't want to see me?

Zara could be wrong, or had Nancy been talking about me to her daughter?

Maybe she had and it was all good, which was why Zara encouraged me to make the ride.

But then again, Nancy was with her work colleagues. There was a chance she wouldn't want to be seen with a biker in front of them. Yeah, there was a high chance she wanted to ignore my sleazy arse. Be too embarrassed I was there, creeping on her in front of her people.

Fuck. I suddenly felt like I did back in my nerdy teen years, so damn unsure about myself.

I'd just have to play it cool. I didn't want to embarrass her in any damn way, so I'd stand back and if she saw me, waved me over or came over to me, I'd then know things were cool with me popping up to Ballarat. If she saw me and then it showed she didn't want anything to do with me, I'd head out to my ride and lick my wounds all the bloody way home.

Sweat started to form on the back of my neck. I was a bundle of fucking nerves—worried she enjoyed texting me rather than wanting to see me face-to-face.

I wanted to run for the exit, but my feet moved me towards the bar. There I ordered two beers, the first I sculled before I took the other in hand and turned to face the room.

Yeah, the lighting was shit, but at least I could still make out the people. It helped me spot the group in the corner booth just as Nancy, who sat on the edge, threw her head back in laughter. She took all the attention. People smiled as they watched her. They even laughed with her because she made it catchy.

Fuck, she was stunning.

She wore jeans, a tee, and her thick hair was up in a messy bun. All I wanted to do was walk over there and take it down, run my fucking fingers through her sexy-as-hell locks.

When she slapped the table and said something else that made others laugh, a smile crept onto my lips as I leaned back against the bar with my arse on one of the stools.

Damn, I could watch her the whole night and not get bored.

Except it was then a dickhead from across the table reached out and placed his hand on Nancy's arm. I tensed, my eyes narrowing onto that hold.

How fucking dare he touch her without Nancy giving the

go-ahead. Christ, I could tell the way she glanced down with a slight frown she wasn't down with having his touch on her.

I fucking hummed in need to go over there and punch the motherfucker in the face.

It was lucky she pulled her arm free and gave him a polite smile, saying something back to whatever he'd said. The other two women at the table shared a look before one of them grabbed Nancy's attention. Frowning, the guy sat back in the booth. I was back to grinning since he'd just been put in his place. It was whether he was going to be stupid and try again that concerned me. Then I would intervene.

Someone stepped up to my side. "Hey, handsome. I'd love to have a drink with you."

I didn't even bother looking at her. My eyes stayed glued to Nancy. "Not interested."

I heard a huff and then retreating footsteps.

It was then Nancy looked my way.

Her eyes widened, then softened. Best of all, she smiled so damn big at the sight of me.

Smirking, I winked, lifted my beer bottle, and tipped it her way before taking a sip.

My chest expanded when her hand lifted and waved me over.

Yeah, my woman was happy to see me.

CHAPTER FIVE

NANCY

*U*sually being at the bar with Kari and Vanessa, my friends and fellow nurses, would be something I'd enjoy a lot. The only dampener on the afternoon sat across from me and next to Kari. Doctor Hendrick called us over as we headed out of the hospital. When he asked what we were up to and we told him, he invited himself along. Which was fine, for the most part. The issue was all he did was talk about himself and apparently, he thought he was pretty damn amazing. He was nice enough, but kind of a douche.

He was blocking my time with my girlfriends and our usual talk about penis size, *Married at First Sight*, and all the strange cases we had to deal with for the week.

I'd just finished telling them a funny story and laughing when Hendrick's, whose first name I didn't even know, hand landed down on my arm.

I swear my stomach rolled.

There went my effort at trying to gain back the night from Doctor Boring.

Nance, this guy's a loser. I smirked from Richard's voice flowing through my mind.

"So, Nancy, since I know you have like a billion paid vacation days, if you could pick anywhere in the world, where would you go?" Vanessa asked to break the awkward silence.

That was simple.

"To be with my girl Josie. Help her get ready for the birth."

"Isn't she away with her two men? Lucky woman."

Smiling, I nodded. "She is. Still, I'd just head to Caroline Springs. I have other friends there."

Also a certain biker who I texted with every day. One who could always draw out a pleasant reaction from me when I saw his name on my screen.

Nothing like Hendrick's.

"Your daughter's with two men?" the douche said with his nose in the air.

I was about to bite back, letting him know she was and how much love she had in her life, when Kari spoke. "Nancy, I think that guy at the bar is staring at you."

I glanced to her and found her pointing towards the bar. Turning, I looked across the room, and my heart stalled.

Roman.

Roman was there, sitting at the bar in Ballarat.

A smile came over me at seeing, actually *seeing* him. He winked my way, smirked, and took a sip of his beer. My hand came up and before my brain registered the move, I was waving him over. *Now, he I could see you with, Nance.* God, was it really Richard's voice or was it my own conscience? I didn't know, but what I did realise was I couldn't seem to stop smiling at seeing Roman. My belly was a flutter of nerves and excitement.

"Don't call that man over, Nancy. He's riff-raff."

"I think he's quite edible," Kari commented.

I said nothing, though I did agree with Kari. I didn't miss the appreciative sigh Vanessa shared. I watched Roman stand. He twisted to put the empty bottle on the bar before facing us again and making his way slowly over.

My stomach dipped and twirled around at the sight of him in his jeans, black tee that covered his broad chest and big arms, biker boots, and his club vest. He may look rough, but it was in a way I admired.

The man had been on my mind constantly. He lessened the sorrow in my heart and replaced it with a different beat.

One just for him it seemed.

How crazy was that?

Not crazy at all, sweetheart.

I shook off Richard's voice and still thought it was completely crazy really, but at that moment seeing Roman in the flesh, I didn't give two shits.

He stood beside the booth and stared down at me, grinning, while I looked up at him smiling like a maniac.

"You're in Ballarat," I stupidly commented.

"Sure am, darlin'."

Darling. No that wasn't right. *Darlin'.* Now that I liked. So did my pulse.

Vanessa dropped another sigh while Kari giggled.

"Who might you be, young man?" Hendrick cut in.

Roman ignored him. Instead, he said, "Scoot over, honey." His chin lifted my way. I glanced behind me to see Vanessa had already moved over. I shifted along, and Roman sat next to me. He didn't face forward though. No, he moved so he had an arm resting along the back of the booth behind me, his other folded on the table, and his eyes stayed glued to me.

His gorgeous blue eyes.

God, could I really think of his eyes that way?

Someone who was so much younger than I was?

I didn't know, but I couldn't help it. Not when he was looking at me with warmth in them.

"How was your day?" he asked. His lips twitched. I caught the movement by watching his mouth move, which was surrounded by a goatee and moustache.

"Good," I whispered, though it wasn't. It was busy and hard, but that didn't matter. I was good right then.

"Glad," he said, as his eyes roamed my face.

"Excuse me, I asked who you were," Hendrick grumbled.

Again, Roman didn't glance away from me. "I'm whoever Nancy says I am to her."

My chest tightened.

"Nancy?" Hendrick demanded.

I briefly glanced at Hendrick, then back, and gulped. "He's Ro—"

"Gamer," Roman said with a smile.

A smile I responded with my own. "Gamer."

"And?" Hendrick snapped.

"He's a friend," I replied, searching Roman to see if I'd hurt him in some way with my response, though I honestly didn't know what he was to me, *yet*.

However, Roman smiled. His hand lifted off the table and gently, his fingers traced the side of my neck. "Yeah, I'm her friend."

I thinned my lips to stop from making a pleased noise as he bit his bottom lip while he watched his fingers on my neck. He traced them up and across my jaw before dropping his hand again.

"Dear Jesus, I think I just came," I heard from Vanessa.

"I'm right there with you," came from Kari.

Good God, I needed new friends right in that moment.

Roman's eyes lit with humour.

"Nancy, how can you associate with men like this, *this*, hooligan?"

Vanessa snorted behind me. Kari laughed out, "Hooligan."

Anger built inside of me. First he judged my daughter and now Roman. It wasn't nice. In fact, it pissed me off. Facing Hendrick, I said harshly, "I think it's time you go, you judgemental arsehole."

"Nancy!" he gasped.

"No," I snapped. "My daughter, who you turned your nose up at, is an amazing, beautiful woman who lived in hell, came out alive, and found the love of two men who absolutely adore her. From what I can see, you'll only see the love of your hand unless you change your attitude and some poor suspecting woman will fall for you." I glared. "And don't you sit there judging the man next to me. I haven't felt lightness in my heart in such a long time. My kids were the only ones bringing me joy until Roman showed me there was more to life after losing Richard. He's kind, sweet, funny, and damn dangerous. So you don't want to piss me off again or I'll let him at you." My chest heaved with every heavy breath I took.

Heat appeared on the back of my neck, Roman's hand calming me.

Hendrick stood. "Don't expect me to speak or be pleasant to you,"—he glared at my friends—"or any of you again."

"Fine with me, jackarse," Vanessa said with a wave.

"Oh, and don't think you can screw us nurses over in the hospital when I know things about you no one should ever know," Kari told him.

He blanched, turned, and stalked off.

"Kari, what do you have on Hendrick?" Vanessa asked.

Kari laughed. "Nothing, but he's obviously been up to something to get the fear of God in his eyes."

I glanced to Roman. His eyes were already on me. His jaw ticked and he nodded. He would look into the doctor in case whatever Hendrick had been up to was harmful to others.

When we didn't look away from one another, Vanessa cleared her throat. "So," she drew out. I startled and shifted back in the seat, so I didn't have my back to her. "How did you and... Gamer, was it?" I nodded. "Meet? By the way, I'm Vanessa and that's Kari."

Roman nodded at both with a smirk on his lips. "Nice to meet ya."

"How did you two meet?" she asked eagerly.

"Um," I started. I side-glanced Roman, hoping he would supply the answer. Only he leaned back in the booth and watched me. Great. "Through my son-in-law and his big family." Usually, I would tell them about everything in life. However, I hadn't mentioned Roman and his attention towards me. I wanted it to stay private for a little longer. My eyes widened a little when I realised I didn't want him to think he was nothing to me. "We've been talking for a while now through text."

"Really," was drawn out by Kari. When I glared at her, I watched her brows raise up and down quickly.

Roman chuckled beside me. "Your girls are as bad as the pussy posse."

Vanessa coughed through a sip of her drink. "The what?"

I started laughing, but managed to explain, "It's what Talon calls Zara's girlfriends." Smiling, I looked at Roman. "Though Julian has a different name altogether."

He snorted. "That he does."

"What?" Kari asked.

"The muffkateers," I said. We all cackled over it. "Or was it another brother who thought of it?"

"Not sure, darlin'. Before my time."

"Before your time? You certainly don't look old." Vanessa commented.

"Meanin' the Ballarat Charter started it," Roman said.

"You're not from there?"

"Nah, Caroline Springs."

"Hmm, that's not far," Vanessa said and looked at me. I rolled my eyes, understanding her look all too well. She could see the interest Roman had in me, though it wasn't hard since he was sitting as close as he could, and his hand was still at the back of my neck.

Roman chuckled. "Not far at all."

"Anyway, Vanessa and I have to get going." Kari scooted along the seat. My eyes widened and my heart raced. They were leaving me with Roman. Alone. My hands started to shake, and anticipation thrummed through me. I was also excited to have time with just him in person instead of over text.

Kari stood beside the booth as Roman got up, his hand coming out. I looked at it and prayed he didn't see how my own trembled as I took his hand. Wordlessly, he helped me stand to let Vanessa out.

"It was great to meet you." Vanessa smiled. Out the corner of her mouth, she muttered, "We'll be talking." I got a quick hug from her before she stood back and Kari came in to wrap her arms around me.

"I like him, Nancy," she whispered. She pulled away and we smiled softly at each other.

"We'll talk soon," I promised them before they walked off.

We stood for a moment longer watching them leave,

though when I glanced to Roman, his eyes were already on me. Again. Was it extra hot in here? It suddenly felt it.

"You cool to stay longer?"

"Yes." I nodded.

His smile was sweet. "Good." He tipped his chin at the booth, and I slid back in. When I didn't feel him sit back down, I looked up and found him leaning forward with his hands on the table. "Get you a drink. What'd you fancy?"

"Um, Coors?"

"Beer woman, my kinda lady." He winked, straightened, and walked off. Of course I watched him go—the sight was amazing—but then I felt guilty for looking, and got pissed at myself for feeling guilty. I was allowed to look. He made sure I knew he was interested, so what was wrong with me looking and being... interested?

I wasn't hurting Richard in any way. If he was still looking down on me, Richard would always know he had my whole heart.

It was just that Roman had started sinking in there as well. I didn't think I was in love with the man. I knew I wasn't. I hardly knew him beyond the texts we'd shared. But I did like him.

Nodding to myself, I finally let acceptance soak into me.

It *was* okay for me to be there with Roman, for me to look, to like, to *like* a lot. Yep, there was nothing wrong about it at all.

I was a grown woman. I could do what I wanted, look at whom I wanted and act however I wanted. Right then, the only issue I could think of that could cause distance between us was the age gap. Especially when a young woman just approached him at the bar. She leaned in and whispered in his ear. My belly sank to the pit of my vagina.

I swallowed hard when he turned his head her way with a sneer on his face and said something to make the woman glare and storm off.

I wanted to clap, to hug him and tell him how much I appreciated seeing that.

When he approached the table though, I said nothing except smiled up at him.

"Here you go, darlin'." He passed me my drink and then slid in next to me. He didn't pick the other side of the booth, but next to me with his arm at the back of where I sat and the other holding his own beer. "Now tell me what you been up to."

I did. I told him about my day, about my grandkids and what they got up to, how Cody had a girlfriend, and that Talon was proud, but how he hated it when Maya came home just yesterday and said she had a boyfriend. He'd grounded her until Zara told him to stop being an arse.

"I'm going to their place for dinner tomorrow night to see the action when Maya brings this poor boyfriend home to meet her parents."

Roman chuckled. "Poor kid. But then again, I'd be fumin' too."

I narrowed my eyes at him, he chuckled again. "Why?"

"She's his baby girl. Doesn't want to see her grow, and really, no kid will be good enough for her."

"True, but he can't be one way for Cody and then another for Maya."

He shrugged, like he thought Talon had every right to be that way.

"Roman!"

He smirked. "Relax, it's the way of men. Wasn't Richard like that with Matthew and Zara?"

At the sudden drop of Richard's name, I tensed. Roman felt it since his hand had strayed to the back of my neck again.

He studied me. "Nancy, you don't want me to mention Rich?"

"No, it's... no. I mean, I was surprised by it. That's all."

His fingers massaged my neck. "You sure?"

Was I?

"Yes." I nodded.

"Good. Bound to happen the more time we talk or spend time together because he was a big part of your life."

"I know."

"But just tell me if I say shit you don't want to talk about."

With courage, I reached out and placed my hand on his thigh under the table and gave it a squeeze. When his eyes bore down on my hand, I went to move it away until he quickly grabbed it and pulled it back over his thigh. His hand applied pressure on mine.

He looked up and grinned. Relaxing back in the seat, he asked again, "Did Rich have a different opinion on your kids?"

I shook my head. "No, he was fine with both of them dating."

"Knew he wouldn't. He was a good man. Though, he was different to what we are."

"We?"

"The brothers of Hawks. We're protective to the point of being possessive."

Smiling, I said, "That's true."

This was what I liked: talking, seeing, feeling him, and finding out who he was. And he was so different from Richard, which I was more than happy with, it seemed.

CHAPTER SIX

GAMER

"Speaking of bein' protective. That dickhead from before, he wants in your pants, Nancy."

I was surprised to see a blush coating her cheeks. "He does, well… did. But he would never."

"No?" I asked, liking hearing her say the fucker would never get in there. Did she know I wanted in there eventually? I reckon she did, and it made me fucking pleased as punch she didn't voice I wouldn't get a chance to slide into her.

Fuck, I hadn't stopped thinking of it since her hand was still on my thigh, even when I'd taken my hand away to gulp my drink down.

"No," she whispered, a brighter heat to her cheeks, which made me wonder if she was thinking along the same lines as I was.

"Good," I stated gruffly like a damn Neanderthal. "I'm gonna find out what the fucker's up to. I'll let you know when I do, but wanna make sure you'll steer clear of him." I grinned like a fool. "Though I have a feelin' he will after the lecture you just gave him." She laughed, only to stop when I reached up and tucked a stray hair behind her ear and to trail my fingers down her neck, up again to along her chin. "Was fuckin' happy to see you have my back, beautiful."

More heat hit her cheeks.

"I, ah, he… annoyed me, and then I was on a roll and…." She shrugged. I tapped her nose with one finger and rested my hand back down over hers on my thigh.

"Whatever it was, fuckin' liked hearin' it."

"Okay," she uttered.

I grinned. "Okay." I paused. "Might sound like a creeper, but been watchin' you, Nancy. Like you loud, funny as fuck, and serious. But I like seein' you get shy for me, darlin', because that, I didn't expect."

She bit her bottom lip, scraped her top teeth over it and then admitted, "I've never really been this way, Roman. You bring it out."

Leaning towards her, I told her, "I fuckin' like that too, Nancy." Seeing her pulse racing, I moved back a bit and picked up my beer, and hoped she liked me admitting it. When I felt her hand tighten on my thigh, I knew she had.

She cleared her throat. "Tell me something about you, Roman."

Fuck.

I hated talking about myself, but for Nancy, I would.

"What you wanna know, sweetheart?"

"Anything. By the way, the nicknames are better."

I chuckled. "Thought I'd try the few normal ones out, but I found your eyes flaring at darlin'."

"They did?" she quietly asked, then licked her lips.

"Yeah, darlin'." I smiled. "Just like that. Now, you wanna know somethin' about me?"

"Yes."

"I joined the Hawks when I was sixteen. Usually they don't take on prospects that young, but the old prez saw what skills I had with a computer. He got me to do shit I wished I never had to. Yet it was a better place than my home life."

"Roman," she whispered, her feelings showing in my name. She felt bad for me.

I ran my fingers up and down the back of her neck, enjoying the shiver from my touch. "Don't feel bad, babe. You live, you learn, and you make sure at the end of it all, your life is how you want it. I'm happy where I am, with the brothers I have, the club I'm in, and with the woman at my side."

Her lips parted. Her nostrils flared on the heavy breath she took. Wasn't sure if it was a good breath or not from what I'd said.

Fear spiked inside of me. "Did I take the last part too far, too soon?"

She shook her head, opened her mouth, closed it, then opened it again and said, "No, Roman. It wasn't too far or too soon. It's good to know."

"We take this at your pace, Nancy. You wanna stay friends, we will."

She smiled warmly. "Friends don't usually touch each other like, well, this."

"Christ, woman, so fuckin' glad I came here, heard you say that, means you're on board with this. At your pace," I reassured again.

"At my pace."

We stayed at the pub until after midnight just talking and getting to know each other better. I fucking loved every damn second of it. She stunned me with how damn beautiful she was. The night was effortless as she made me laugh, relax, and enjoy the time with her.

I didn't want to see her gone, but when she kept yawning, I knew our time was going to have to come to an end. Since I didn't trust that doctor dickhead, I told her I was following her home. She put up a little bit of a fight, but in the end, conceded when I told her it'd give me peace of mind.

I pulled my ride up behind her car in the driveway and climbed off. She was already out of the car by the time I made it to her side.

I took her keys out of her hand, then grabbed her hand in my free one and led her up to her door. Unlocking it, I told her, "Wait here for me."

"Roman—"

I dropped her hand to grip the side of her neck. "Nancy, humour me, yeah?"

"Okay."

"Okay." I grinned.

Stepping in, I switched on the hall light, and made my way through the house, searching every room. Something didn't rub me right about the doctor, so I was going to go with my gut and make sure my woman's place was safe before I left her.

It wasn't something I wanted to do, but I had to.

I could tell she'd want to know the ins and outs of me and my life before moving onto being more serious, and I was down with that. I totally understood it. As far as I knew, she'd had one man between her legs and in her life.

Hell, if she wasn't ready until a year down the track, I'd still be there waiting. I knew she'd be worth it.

I stepped back out the front to a smiling Nancy. Shit, it was good to see her smiling at me.

"All good, darlin'."

"Thank you," she said, her hand fidgeting on her bag in front of her.

"Anythin' for you. I better hit the road."

"Are you riding back tonight?" she asked with worry in her tone.

"Nah, I'm gonna head to the compound here and crash. I' head off in the mornin'. Got shit to do back home."

"Okay." She nodded. "Good, I didn't want you riding so late

Fucking cute.

"You didn't?" I asked, reaching out to land my hands on he hips.

Her breath caught. "N-no."

"Like you worryin' about me, Nancy. Wish I had time to se you tomorrow."

"Soon?" she asked, gazing up at me with what looked lik hope in her eyes.

"Yeah, darlin'. Soon." I looked over her head, then bac down into her eyes. "Gotta go."

"Okay," she whispered.

"All right." I nodded, but didn't move. We stood staring each other for a moment longer, cars drove by, an owl hootee and it wasn't until I saw her eyes flicker down to my lips that knew I was good to go. Leaning in, I pressed my lips to th corner of her mouth. There, I said, "Text me when you wake."

Her voice was shaky when she replied, "I will."

I straightened, dropped my hands, and stepped back. "Ha a good night, Nancy."

"So did I, Roman."

I winked. "Glad. Head in, darlin'. Wanna hear the lock."

She nodded. Still smiling, she stepped into her house an

when I heard her do as I asked—lock her door—I made my way to my ride.

When I was on, kicking my ride to life, I heard, "Roman."

Looking up, I watched Nancy running my way. Quickly, I turned off my bike and got off, reaching out for her as she collided with my front.

"What is it?" I demanded, on alert.

"Nothing." She shook her head. "It's just... I, ah, thank you. For coming to see me."

My chest inflated in elation. My shoulders dropped, relaxing after the fear fled my mind and body.

"Anytime you wanna see me, Nancy, I'll be here."

She didn't say anything, only stared up at me.

"Somethin' else?" It looked like something was playing on her mind.

"Yes," she admitted.

"What, darlin'?"

"It wasn't enough."

My head jerked back slightly. "Sorry?" Confusion had my brows dipping.

"It wasn't enough," she said again.

"What wasn't?"

She shook her head. Then, fuck me to hell and back, she got to her toes. Her hand ran up my chest to cup behind my neck, and she pulled my shocked self down enough to touch her lips to mine.

She started a fire inside of me with her lips against mine.

My arms wrapped around her tightly, one at her waist the other at the back of her head, and she opened for me. I growled into her mouth at first taste. Christ, she could kiss. What she meant, my small kiss wasn't enough for her, finally

LILA ROSE

sank in. She wanted more from me. Wanted my taste. The first taste of her new man.

I was all for it.

Fuck, having her pressed against me, with her hands on my body was more than I imagined. What made it the goddamn best night was when her hand started sneaking down my waist to my arse. There she squeezed, only to gasp against my lips and remove herself altogether.

Still, I didn't mind. Her lust-filled eyes and her heaving chest were enough to tell me she enjoyed that kiss just as much as I did.

"Sorry, I didn't mean to grab you like that," she said, then laughed. "Actually, I did."

Chuckling, I dragged her back into me with my hands at the back of her neck. "Glad you got carried away. But I know if we start again, I won't want to leave. One last quick one for the road, darlin'."

She sighed. "I suppose."

I laughed. "Fuckin' beautiful. You wantin' more of me is the damn best feelin', Nancy."

Her brows pulled together. "It is?"

"Yeah, I'd show you just how much, but that'd lead to other things."

Her eyes widened, understanding she'd got me hard. Grinning, I took her mouth again in a rough, wet, but short kiss.

Damn it was hard to pull away. Yet I did. Then I turned her. "Let me watch you walk away, darlin'. Lock your door and wave to me at your window."

"I guess I should."

Snorting out a laugh, I kissed the side of her neck. "Night, Nancy."

"Night, Roman." She sighed and it sounded like a happy one. Shit, I brought that out in her. Me.

NANCY

In a daze, I walked back into the house. Locking the door after me, I made my way to the window. Parting the curtain, I waved. I probably looked like a lunatic with how much I was smiling, but I didn't care. I waited until he was out of sight before I moved into the kitchen. There I gripped the counter tightly to hold me up.

That kiss.

It was more than I thought it would be.

I still couldn't believe I'd done it, but it annoyed me that all I'd got was a peck when I'd wanted more.

I'd wanted more.

From another man.

Guilt blew through me. I couldn't help my attraction, but I still felt I was doing wrong by Richard.

Enough of that, Nance. Coolness touched my back, and my eyes widened. *You need to feel free again. Get back what you lost when I left. Be the horndog, ball-busting woman I loved. Don't feel guilty, sweetheart. Enjoy your life.*

Could I do that?

I wanted to... but—

No buts, Nance.

Maybe it was time to find the person I was before.

Maybe it was time to cherish what I had, enjoy life, and live each day to its fullest.

Though, if I got kisses like that one from Roman all the time, I knew I would enjoy each day.

My heart raced at the thought of being with Roman, of the possibility of us being together. Dating.

Was I worried about what people thought when seeing Roman with me? Yes. Would it be enough for me to back away from Roman? No. I wanted him, and no matter how people reacted, I would put it aside because being with him made *me* happy. That was all I had to think about.

CHAPTER SEVEN

GAMER

Somehow I managed to not run into Talon while I was in Ballarat, and I was goddamn grateful for it. It was a few days later—a few days where I missed Nancy like crazy since I'd been damn spoilt having her in my arms—that I got a phone call from the big boss man.

I sat in the computer room going through some shit bookwork while Jason sat at the other desk watching the security videos of the strip clubs the Hawks owned. When my phone rang, I stared down at it and the name flashing on the screen, and all I could think was fuck.

"You gonna get it?" Jason asked.

"Not sure."

He laughed. "Who is it?"

"Talon."

His eyes widened. "You'd better get it."

"Yeah, you're right." I picked it up. "Prez, what can I do for you?"

He growled into the phone, "You wanna fuckin' tell me,

Gamer, why in the fuck you were in Ballarat and didn't hang 'round to see me?"

"Just thought I'd pop in, see the lay of the land. You'd invited me a while ago and never took you up with it. Got in late though and had to leave early. Next time I'll stay longer to see your smilin' face."

"Do. Not. Motherfuckin'. Play. With. Me. You saw her, didn't you?" he snarled down the line, loud enough for Jason to turn back around with wide eyes.

I gave him the thumbs up. "Who?"

"Gamer, I'm gonna reach out here and ask you be goddamn honest with me and I'll cool my temper and let this mishap slide, with you not tellin' me of your visit."

"Be honest?"

"Yeah, brother. You got that in you?"

"I got a lotta respect for you Talon. A helluva lot. You got Hawks into a path we can all be proud of. You take care of all the brothers like they are your blood. So I'm gonna give it to you honest like. Not only because of that, but because of your mother-in-law. Yeah, I came up to see Nancy because she's it for me. Not sure you're gonna handle that well, but I'm hopin' for her sake one day you will."

"You've laid it out good and proper there, Gamer." *Shit, this doesn't sound good.* "Now you gotta listen to me. Nancy means a helluva lot to me. She's my woman's mother. She's the grand-mother to our kids. She had a good man. She doesn't need anyone in his place. She's happy. I won't have you fuck her 'round."

I sighed. I didn't expect him to accept my place in her world right away. "You honestly think she's completely happy?" I didn't let him answer, I went on. "Then you didn't see what I did. Only now she's happier with me in her life."

"Gamer—"

"Talon, Prez, respect, you have it all. But don't come between me and *my* woman."

"What the fuck you—"

I ended the call and turned off my phone.

Jason whispered, "He's gonna kill you."

"Yeah, I reckon you could be right."

"You should go into hidin'. Me ma has a spare room."

I smiled. "Thanks, brother, but I'm gonna see how this'll play out. Won't look good if he can't find me to give me an arse kickin'."

He nodded. "True. I'll try and get him to go easy on you."

"Thanks, brother."

"You're a good man, Gamer. Taught me heaps."

With a chin lift in appreciation, I said, "Better get back to watchin', Jase."

He gave me a salute. "Will do." He spun around in his seat with a smile. Over his shoulder, he added, "It'd really suck if Talon kills you."

I chuckled. "Brother, I think I may just scrape by with Nancy and Zara at my back."

"Oh yeah, he listens to them most of the time. Well, mainly Wildcat."

I sure as fucking hoped he still did.

NANCY

The cafeteria was bustling with patients, family members, nurses, and doctors. In line to purchase some food, my phone rang. Pulling it out of my pocket, I smiled when I saw Zara's name on the screen.

"Hello, daughter of mine."

"Mum, listen to me really quick. I tried to stop him, told him to wait until you finished work, but he's in a snit and on his way to you."

"Who?" I asked.

"Talon. He's worried Gamer's taking advantage of you. He learnt Gamer was in town and knows he was here to see you. He called Gamer—"

"Zara—"

"I know, I know. I tried to tell him to mind his own business, but you know my man. He's up in everyone's life."

A murmur started in the sitting area. I dropped my head knowing it would be my son-in-law with his biker gear gaining the attention of everyone.

"He's here."

"Shit, I'm on my way—"

"Honey, don't worry. We'll have dinner tomorrow night still, but I'll sort Talon out today."

"Good luck."

"I won't need it," I answered, and hung up.

The chatter got louder around me; it was how I knew he was close. Still, I stayed in the line and waited for him to find me. I wouldn't get embarrassed to have my son-in-law there wanting to grill me. I didn't care what people thought about who my family was, even when he looked like he could murder someone with a glare.

"Nancy," was growled out. I glanced over to see him in the doorway with his arms crossed over his chest and Griz standing at his side. "A word," he bit out.

I sighed. "I can't right now. I'm in the line and if I lose my spot—"

"Griz," Talon ordered. Griz stomped forward, took my tray and with a hand on my back, he gently pushed me Talon's way while he took my spot in line.

"Fine," I muttered, rolling my eyes. I was sure everyone around us was staring, wondering who Talon and Griz were to me. "Nothing to see here. Just a pain-in-the-butt son-in-law sticking his nose in where it's not needed."

Griz chuckled behind me while Talon clipped, "Nancy."

Just to annoy him, I made my way over slowly. Once I was close, he took my arm and pulled me along behind him out into the eating area where more people stared. We kept going. I waved to a few nurses I knew. They seemed concerned, so I called, "It's all right. He's family."

When my eyes landed on Doctor Hendrick's, I noticed how pale he was. He seemed more scared of Talon than he did Roman. Then again, maybe he just didn't take notice of Roman's vest that night.

I wondered if Roman had had any luck finding out Hendrick's secret. At least it was an excuse to call him later, other than to find out how Talon treated him.

Talon stopped in a corner, far enough away not to be overheard. He dropped my arm, spun towards me, and crossed his arms over his chest, glaring down.

I scoffed. "Don't give me that disappointed look, son-in-law. It only works on the kids, not me. I also have nothing to be sorry for."

"Nance—"

"No. Talon, I love you with all my heart. You've been a godsend for my daughter, but I won't have you trying to run my life. I like Roman. I want to see where it goes with him. I know you loved Richard like he was your father and don't want to see another at my side because of him, but don't you think I deserve some more happiness in life? Even if it comes from another man."

His jaw clenched. "I didn't know you were unhappy, Nancy."

Reaching out, I put my hand on his arm. "I wasn't happy, but I made sure to try and be because I have a beautiful family. It wasn't until Roman that I realised there was something missing. Something that could bring me more joy in life than my family."

"He's club."

My brows dipped. "Does that mean there's a rule against club members for me?"

"You're my mother-in-law. You deserve more—"

"Pish-posh. Don't pull that bullshit either. The men in the club are more and better men than others I've met. That's because you've taught them well. I know you don't want to hear this about a brother, but Roman is sweet, caring, and willing to see where this goes with me, at *my* pace."

A vein ticked in his forehead. "I don't fuckin' like it, Nancy. You could get hurt."

My heart softened, and I knew my eyes had when he looked at me. He started to relax. "I know I could, my son-in-law. However, it's a risk *I'm* willing to take in *my* life."

"Jesus, woman, just think for a moment longer before you sell your heart into it. He's younger. He's—"

My hand came up in his face. "First, do not call me woman. Second, he *is* younger and that's a worry I'll bear, but he's proven himself, in my eyes, to be serious about me being an older lady. Also… Griz and Deanna, Warden and Emerson. We won't be the only ones with an age gap. Lastly, have some trust in us, Talon. Whatever Roman and I have growing won't interfere in the club."

"I just don't want to see you get hurt." His jaw clenched again. It was sweet how much he cared, but I knew a big part of it would be because he saw it as me moving on from Richard. Those two had a bond so big it was amazing. I didn't like hurting him by starting something with Roman, but I had agonised over it so much myself. Finally, I knew life was worth living and loving as many people in it as you could before God chose it was your time to pass.

"Thank you, my handsome son-in-law. Richard would be proud of you taking care of me, but he would also want me to do what I want, and right now, it's me giving a chance to Roman. If things don't work out, it won't be the end of the world. I'll know it wasn't meant to be. It may hurt, a lot, but I can take it, Talon. I can take it because I know I have so much support at my back."

His nostrils flared. "Fuck," he snarled. "Okay."

I tried to hide the smile, but I couldn't. "Glad to have your permission to do what I want to do in my life."

He nodded. His lips twitched before he tipped his chin up and looked over my shoulder. "That fucker starin' at you, he a problem?"

I glanced over my shoulder to see Hendrick quickly look away. "No. He's an idiot. Besides, Roman's already onto it."

"Good."

Griz stepped up to our sides. "Your tray's on the table, Nancy."

"Thanks, handsome. How're the monsters?"

Griz grinned. "Good."

"I'm glad," I said, patting his arm. I faced Talon again and told him, "You're not leaving without laying one on me, son-in-law."

"Christ," he muttered. Yet he still leaned in and kissed me on my cheek.

"Before you go, will you promise to leave Roman alone?"

He laughed; it was kind of dark. "That's the thing, Nancy. He's Hawks. I'll be makin' sure he knows what's right."

"Talon—"

"See you tomorrow night for dinner," he said before stalking off with Griz.

Well, I think I sort of won. Which made me smile.

CHAPTER EIGHT

GAMER

"Would you come here for a club family day?" I asked with my fucking heart in my throat. It was a big step, a big deal. I wasn't sure if Nancy would know, but you only brought women you were serious about to club family days.

"Me?" she whispered into the phone.

I forced a laugh. "Yeah, I don't hear anyone else on the line."

"Tomorrow?"

"Yeah, darlin'. You're not workin', right? I got your schedule you sent me a couple days ago right in front of me. Unless, fuck, do you have somethin' else planned? You goin' somewhere with your girls?"

"Um, no, I would like to come, if you're sure?"

"I'm sure, Nancy."

"Okay," she breathed. Yeah, she knew family club day was important.

"While I got you on the line, I got some news about that dickhead doctor."

"Is it bad?"

Laughter erupted out of me. "Nah, darlin'. Just fuckin' weird, which is probably why he doesn't want it to get out."

"What is it?"

"He goes to a club every now and then."

"A club? That doesn't sound weird. Although, is it a sex club?"

"Nope. It's a cross-dressin' kinda club. The dude likes to wear women's clothes as he gets on stage and mimes to songs."

Her laughter drifted down the line. "No wonder he was looking scared when Talon showed and practically dragged me out of the room—"

"What?" I snarled, gripping my phone tightly to my head as anger reared inside of me. President or not, no fucker touches my woman like that. "He manhandled you? What the fuck for?"

"Roman," she said in a tone that made her sound like she was pleased, yet like I'd said something funny. "Relax, it wasn't as it sounds. He's worried about us. As in you and me. However, we talked it out. He understands I want to see where things will go for us. He's just worried I'll get hurt. Especially with you being younger—"

A growl left my lips. "You don't need to worry about anythin' with me. He doesn't need to get up in your grill about this shit between us. I'd damn shoot myself before hurtin' you in any damn way. I don't fuckin' look at anyone but you, Nancy. Fuck the age gap. It shouldn't be between us because to me, I don't goddamn see one."

All I could hear was her breathing on the other end.

"Nancy?"

"I-if you were here, I would kiss you," she said softly.

Christ.

"Then I wish I was there, darlin'."

"I'll see you tomorrow, Roman."

"Tomorrow, you want me to drive up and pick you up?"

She laughed. "No, I'm pretty sure I can manage to drive down there. Um… do you live at the compound?"

Fuck me. It was then I wished I didn't, wondering if she wanted to stay the night. I didn't offer, thinking it was too soon.

"Yeah, I do. Have since I got in, but I'm lookin' for a place to settle."

"It's okay. I was just wondering. I can understand not wanting to move out of a place that's convenient for you. I'll be there around ten. Is that all right?"

"Sounds good, Nancy. See you here."

"Yes. Bye, Roman."

"Later, darlin'." Ending the call was getting harder and harder each time. Fuck, if I had all day, I'd stay on the phone with her. Somehow glue it to my head. Hell, I was going overboard with thinking that. But the point was, I'd listen to her all day.

Standing, I started for the door when Jason called, "Nancy's comin' tomorrow?"

"Yeah, brother. You gonna be here?"

"Sure will." He grinned. "My woman's lookin' forward to it."

"Good to hear. You two still goin' strong?"

"Always will. She's it for me like it sounds like Nancy is for you."

"That she is, Jase."

"Good. I thought you were into men to start with because I never saw you hook up, but now I know you were just waitin' for your special someone."

Chuckling, I nodded. "Yeah, I was waitin' for my special someone."

"Hell yes to it finally happenin'."

"Damn right."

And there wasn't anyone or anything to stop me from claiming Nancy in all the ways I wanted. It was getting to a time I'd need to make some decisions, not just yet, but damn soon, and I didn't see myself in Caroline Springs much longer.

Just had to pray to everything there was to pray to that Talon would have me in the Ballarat Charter in the future.

The next day I stood out the front waiting for Nancy. The place was already packed with family members getting shit ready for the cookout that'd probably last all day and into the night. I may have been out there waiting for a while, which caused me to get some strange looks from some of the guys until I told them I was waiting on Nancy. Then their looks changed into understanding, and they smirked in a teasing way.

It was only Texas, Dodge's nephew, now really his kid, that said shit. "Gamer and the older lady gonna get it on." I started for him, but stopped when Dodge's hand covered Texas's mouth and dragged him into the compound.

Apparently, Texas was just like Dodge when he was in his teens. A smartarse. Though, ever since Dodge took over as president of this charter, he'd grown a hell of a lot.

"I think it's sweet," Romania, Dodge's niece and yet daughter, said as she skipped alongside Low, Dodge's woman.

"It really is," Low commented with a huge-arse grin.

Just when I was going to reply, I noticed Nancy's hatchback pulling into the car park. I caught her wave and grinned like a fool already on my way over to her. She parked, got out, and sucked in a sharp breath when I saw she had her hair down

She slung her bag over her shoulder, closed her door, and then opened the back door.

Then I got to her. She glanced up from her back seat to me as I wound my arms around her waist. "Fuck, you look stunnin'. Love your hair down, darlin'."

She straightened, turned, and her hands slipped to my chest. "You do?"

"Oh yeah." I nodded.

"How much?"

"A fuckin' lot."

She glanced around. "Are you willing to show me how much with a kiss? Or is that too forward? I've been wanting to kiss you since the last time I did, and seeing you doesn't help that want go away, and there's no one around—"

My lips landed on hers. Her hands climbed to around my neck while I slid one hand from her waist up and straight into her long, thick, and fucking gorgeous hair. I growled into her mouth when she opened for me under my teasing tongue.

We tasted each other. She whimpered, and I sucked it down into me, enjoying the sound, the feel of her.

Pulling back after a quick touch again of her lips against mine, I warned her, "Never care who's around. You kiss me when you want it. You need my mouth, it's always there for you."

"Okay, Roman."

"Good." I watched as I ran my fingers through her hair. "Fuckin' like silk." I looked forward to the day it'd be splayed out on my pillow.

"Has anyone told you how good-looking you are?" she asked.

Grinning, I shrugged. "A few, but no one as important as you." I tugged on her hair, and blood pumped right to my cock when I witnessed her eyes flare in heat. "You like your man's looks?"

She licked her lips, as if still coming down from that one hair pull. "Yes," she whispered.

"Hmm." I kissed her neck. "Enjoy knowin' you think I'm all right for you."

"W-we should head in."

"You gettin' shy on me, darlin'?"

"Yes, no… in a way, um, I like you playing with my hair is all. If we don't move inside, then the back seat of the car looks good to fool around in, but then we'd squish the treats I made for you."

"For me?"

"Well, yes and everyone."

"You cooked thinkin' of me eatin' them?"

"Yes?"

My smile wasn't to be contained. "Takin' care of me without even really knowin' it. You're fuckin' amazin', Nancy Alexander."

Her eyes warmed even more. "So are you, Roman Power."

"Right, I'm wantin' to get these treats in to try, but I'm also thinkin' of foolin' around now."

She tilted her head back, neck stretched as she burst out laughing.

Joy.

There it was in her voice, in her eyes and body as she held onto me while she couldn't contain her mirth.

Joy. She had it and I gave it to her, but I also had it because she gave it to me.

Nothing could make me happier in that moment.

She slapped my chest gently. "You're crazy."

I grinned. "Yeah, I am." For her. I glanced in the back seat. "Jesus, Nancy, how much you think I can eat?"

Again, she was cackling. "I said it's not all for you."

"I don't like to share though."

"Well, you'll have to in this case."

"But no other case."

Her smile was shy. "No."

"Deal then. Now kiss me, and we'll get this shit inside."

She got to her toes, wrapped her arms around my neck and did so smiling. A moment later, she lost her grin as she looked at my lips and leaned in. "I like kissing you, Roman."

"I know the feelin', darlin'," I said, just before our mouths pressed against each other.

Coming up for air, I asked, "You crashin' in town tonight?"

She nodded. "I was going to stay at Josie's while she's out of town."

"Good, wasn't sure how long today will go and didn't want you drivin' back." I shifted back after a kiss to her neck and leaned in the car grabbing as many trays as I could so she wouldn't have to take much. "Though, I'm gonna offer, but you don't have to take it, and I'm not offerin' to get somethin' out of it. You're pace, darlin'."

She leaned into the car herself and grabbed the one tray left. "Offer what?"

"You can stay here, in my room for the night. I could grab a spare one somewhere else."

"You wouldn't mind?"

"No, Nancy."

"Thank you, that would be nice."

"It ain't the cleanest place to sleep in."

She juggled the tray as her fingers pressed against my lips. She shook her head, smiling. "Guys will be guys. This place is full of them. I understand what you're saying, but know I don't care either way."

"All right." I grinned. We started towards the door. "Does Talon know you're down here?"

"No, no one does. Though, I know that won't last long. I wanted to spend time with you in your environment without my family interfering."

Chuckling, I told her, "You do know what you'll be walkin' into right? Just because Wildcat, Hell Mouth, and all the other pussy posse ain't here doesn't mean you won't get bombarded with questions about us."

"Shit. For some reason, I didn't think of that."

"Don't worry, I'll have your back."

She bumped into my side. "I know you will."

CHAPTER NINE

NANCY

*I*t had been years since I felt so light in my body, my soul, my heart. All of me was shining, and it was all because of the man beside me. Yes, I would always and forever miss the man who still held my heart in the fiercest way. Richard was my life. It seemed, though, that Roman could be my oxygen.

No other man had captured my attention like the way Richard had, until Roman. I realised the previous night, knowing where I would be going and how much it meant to a man like Roman, he wouldn't invite me to a family day with the Hawks MC if I didn't mean a whole lot of something to him. What I figured was that our connection wasn't because of Roman paying attention to me first. I wasn't using him. There had been other men who'd asked me to coffee or told me I was pretty, but they hadn't woken me up.

Roman woke me from a deep sleep I hadn't known I was in. It was as if he started my life again.

It was crazy since we'd only been in contact for over a

month, but I felt connected to Roman in a way I couldn't turn away from. I also had a feeling he wouldn't let me either.

Smiling to myself, I said, "I'm looking forward to the day."

He bent enough to capture my lips in a quick kiss. "So am I, darlin'."

Opening the door, I held it open for Roman to enter. His lips thinned and I had to laugh, sure he was annoyed at himself for not being able to have his hands free to open the door for me. However, he had grabbed all trays except one to carry in, so I wouldn't be weighed down.

"Get in there," I ordered.

A single brow rose. "Could get used to you bein' bossy."

Heat rushed to my cheeks since my mind went straight to the bedroom and what type of orders he would take. And then I got embarrassed for even thinking it after only a month. Or was it normal? I didn't have a clue because it had been so long since I'd courted.

Roman noticed my cheek colour and started chuckling. "What you thinkin', Nancy?"

"Nothing," I snapped. Then with a hand to his back, I pushed him through the door; he was still laughing.

As soon as we walked through the second door and into the common area, people surrounded us. Greetings in some ways were supplied by all of them. Those I didn't really know stood back, yet I got a chin lift from those as well.

It felt like I'd been accepted into another family.

All because of the man at my side.

"Here, brother, let me take them off your hands," Dive said to Roman.

Roman twisted in a way Dive couldn't get them and glared at his brother. "Touch them you die."

"Roman, I made them for everyone." I laughed.

"I'll share with the kids, that's about it," he stated, still eyeing his brother.

Dive scoffed. "Koda loves his dad. He'll grab me one."

"I'll word him up. He'll listen to me since I have the game he loves playin'." Roman faced me, leaned in and caught my lips with his in front of everyone. "Gonna put these in the kitchen. Dive, make yourself useful and grab Nancy's tray."

"Then I can have a slice?" Dive asked, smirking.

"I'll see," Roman grumbled. "Be back, yeah?"

"Yes." I smiled. Warmth spread through my chest with his uncertainty about leaving me. However, I could take anything on, especially since I knew the people there and also because I had Roman with me.

He was being ridiculous, in a humorous way, not wanting to share the treats I'd made. I watched as he walked off as Dive quickly swiped my tray from my hands and followed. Still, my eyes stayed on Roman... well, a certain part of him in his hugging jeans.

"You seem transfixed there, Nancy," Low mentioned from my side.

"It's certainly something to be transfixed over," I told her honestly and then glanced to her. Others were around, but not close. Mena was handling Koda while he tried to grab for Vin, Beast's dog. Knife laughed, until Neveah nearly dropped out of his arms when she leapt for the fun times on the floor. "Tell me honestly, Low. Do you think I'm too old for this?"

She studied my face for a moment before calling, "Women, time to gather and talk."

"Low," I warned.

"No, Nancy. You should know from the girls in Ballarat we're up in each other's business and share moments of our lives with each other, like you're about to have with us."

Shit. I shouldn't have said anything.

Mena, Nary, Melissa, a very pregnant Della, Poppy, and her girlfriend, Manda, walked our way. Low took my hand in hers and pulled us towards a corner where there were couches. The men who already sat there glanced up. Low demanded, "Brothers, can you give us this area for some women's business?" Even though they showed their displeasure with a few curses and grumbles, they still moved off.

It just went to show how amazing the Hawks men were with their women.

Low ushered me into the corner, and the others sat around us. "Now, Nancy, ask your question again."

I groaned, glancing around to the much younger women. I wished Kari and Vanessa were there. Then again, they'd tell me how stupid I was being because they could see how much Roman was interested in me. I could see it too, or else I wouldn't be there, but it still worried me I was too old for him.

"It's okay, Nancy. You don't have to share. Low thinks everyone does, but we're not all like that," Mena said.

"You bitches should be." Low glared. She caught my eyes. "You asked if you were too old for this and by this, I'm thinkin' you mean bein' with Gamer. My answer would be no. Shit, woman, I haven't seen Gamer with anyone or even act as if he thought of bangin' one of the club girls. He's all calm and shit. Then BAM, he's all about Nancy."

"Nancy, do you like him?" Della asked.

"Oh, she likes him," Melissa said, smiling. "I saw the way your eyes hungered for his body when he walked away."

Della snorted. "I didn't mean in the looks way. He is good-looking." She glanced over her shoulder. "Don't let Handle know I said that. But what I mean is, and this is just an observation from someone who is fairly new to the club, I've seen you many times. You love your kids and grandbabies, but I also felt there was something missing from you."

Nary nodded. "Something you lost when Richard passed."

"Something you may have gained back since seeing Roman?" Poppy commented. "Because you do seem…."

"Lighter," Low said.

"Happier," Nary added.

"Hornier," Manda put in. We all looked to her. "What? I had to throw something in."

Laughing, I nodded to all of them. "He does make me feel all those things again."

Della shrugged, rubbing her belly. "Then I wouldn't worry if you think you're too old for this. I wouldn't worry about anything if I was feeling all wonderful again in life."

"I agree, and you know no one will judge you here." Mena grinned.

Was that all I'd been worried about, what people thought? While I'd told Talon I didn't care, a small part of me obviously still did. I had to put it aside. They were right. I was happier than I had been in years, and it was because of Roman Power.

"You're all right." I nodded.

"So," was called, all of us jumping at the sudden voice. Low and I turned in our seats to see Julian pop up from behind the couch. "Do you need to set that appointment for a wax yet?" he asked.

Glaring, I grabbed my bag, swung it wide and hit him in the gut. "You scare me like that again, you little shit, and I'll castrate you."

"Oh, come now, mumma bear, you love me too much."

"What're you doing here? Where's my son and grand-daughter?"

"Home. I overheard Zara telling Mattie you were coming

here. Of course I couldn't miss out." He sat on the armrest near me. "Hey, girlfriends, good to see you all." He blew kisses all around, then tapped me on the arm. "You didn't answer me. Do you need an appointment?"

"Don't," Mena breathed.

Low cackled. "Honey, just because your experience was bad doesn't mean it's the same for all."

"I know someone else who would agree with me."

"Yeah, who?" Low asked.

"No one." Mena shook her head, glancing away.

"Mena, there's a story there and I want to know."

"I have to check on Koda," she quickly said and got up, walking away.

Low harrumphed and sat back in the couch.

"Mumma bear," Julian whined. "You haven't answered me."

"Then no, I don't need that done yet."

"Yet." He grinned. The rest of the women did too. When chatter started around us, Julian leaned closer. His arm went around my back. "I also, 100 percent agree with the women. Gamer's good for you. You have nothing to worry about."

Smiling, I nodded. "I get that feeling also."

"Good. Oh, speaking of that delicious hunk of a man, he's storming this way."

Roman was indeed storming our way with a scowl on his face.

Quickly, I stood. "What's wrong?"

"Are they givin' you shit about us?"

Good God, he was worried and ready to battle all of them for me.

"Aww," Julian cooed.

Reaching out, I placed my hand on Roman's chest. "No,

everything's fine." His wild eyes roamed my face. Finally, he nodded.

"You want a drink? Somethin' to eat?"

Sliding my hand down, I took his in mine. "How about I come with you to grab something?"

"Sounds good." His grin was back as he stared down at our hands. Was he seeing what I was trying to show? That no matter what he thought people were saying, bad or good, I would always come back to him.

He'd been nothing but supportive of me and I had to let my doubts about our age difference go because it was holding me back, even when I didn't realise it was.

Together, we walked down the hall towards the kitchen. There we grabbed some drinks, a plate of food, and sat at the table with some of the other brothers I didn't know well. Roman introduced me to them again.

It was Elvis who asked, "You two a thing?"

Roman glanced at me. I nodded to Elvis and said, "Haven't you heard? Once you go old, you're sold."

They all laughed. Roman wrapped his arm around my neck and tugged me into his side. "You're not old. You gotta stop thinkin' that," he whispered into my ear.

Leaning back, I nodded. "I'm going to try."

He kissed me, which brought the catcalls out. With a final breathless peck against my lips, he trailed his nose across my cheek until he said, "Good," against my ear.

CHAPTER TEN

NANCY

*I*t was late by the time Roman, with my bag from the car in his hand, walked me down another hall in the bedroom area. He stopped at a door near the end and opened it.

"This is mine," he said, and waved me through. I stepped in, my eyes widening a little. Why had he been worried about the cleanliness? The place was spotless.

Turning to face him, I smiled and raised my brows in question. He'd already dropped my bag when he rubbed at the back of his neck. "I paid a prospect to clean my shithole up, in case you did agree to stay in here."

Abrupt laughter fell from my mouth. "Next time, don't. I want to see the horrors of how untidy you think you are."

"Darlin', I can get very dirty."

Were we still talking about cleaning?

I know my mind wasn't. Right then, it was on the king-size bed I saw with me laying tied on it while Roman…. I gulped.

I also knew my body had reacted to those words in a different way.

My belly swooped low, my nipples hardened, and I felt a tingle below. It was as if my vagina was saying, "Aye aye, Captain. Ready and present for action."

My cheeks were on fire. I quickly glanced away from a smirking Roman and turned back to the room. Only it was then his heat hit my back and his arms wound around my waist.

Roman rested his chin down on my shoulder. "Maybe another time we can put to action whatever you were thinkin'."

"Um...."

He chuckled. "Come lay with me for a bit?" His hands squeezed my waist before he straightened and let me go. He took off his vest, shoes, and socks.

"Sure," I breathed. After kicking off my shoes and taking off my socks, I went to the right side of the bed and sat down. I pulled my legs up and when Roman climbed on the other side, I slid down to lie next to him as my heart beat like it was a wild beast.

Roman shifted over on his side while I lay on my back. He got up to his elbow and rested his head on his hand, staring down at me with a small smile on his lips. His other hand landed on my belly, which caused me to jump.

"Relax."

I laughed. "I will eventually."

"Have you always wanted to be a nurse?" he asked. His abrupt change of topic was his way of trying to lessen my nerves. It was sweet, and it worked since I loved talking to him about anything and everything.

"Yes. Well, at first, I pictured myself being a veterinarian. When I was a little girl and took a kitten home with a broken leg, I cried and cried because I couldn't fix it. It wasn't until I was older and found my emotions were stronger with people than animals that I knew my life would lead me to being a nurse. If I stayed the course of focussing on animals, I would be crying every day when I couldn't help them."

His expression was serious when I looked up at him. I didn't expect it to be. Worry laced through me. Reaching up, I rested my hand against his cheek. His eyes flashed down to me. "I got a soft spot for animals as well."

"I heard you've claimed Easton's dogs as yours also."

He nodded. "The only thing you don't know is why I'm so easy to connect with animals." He sucked in a breath. "When I was young, I had a heap of dogs. They were my refuge when my dick of a father was, well, being a dick. They'd also been the friends I didn't have at school. Fuck, I sound like an idiot."

"You don't," I tried to reassure him. "How come you don't have any animals now?" I pressed, sensing something behind it.

He stared over me at the wall in thought. "Because it fuckin' killed me when my father made me stand beside him as he shot my dogs in the head all because I didn't take the rubbish out."

Oh God, no.

My stomach plummeted while my heart rate spiked. "Roman," I murmured, running my hand to his neck, over his chest.

"Not gettin' attached," he said, "was how I lived my life." His eyes came back down to me. "I've only recently learned, bein' attached is a good thing. Making connections, puttin' down roots, and livin' a life with people you care about *is* important." He shrugged, as if what he said was nothing. But it wasn't.

My hand slid to the back of his neck and I gently pulled him down so I could have his mouth, his perfect lips against mine.

It started out slow, just a brush of lips before we were grinning against each other's mouths. Only my grin was wiped away when his eyes darkened. His tongue came out to run along my bottom lip. I sucked in a breath as his teeth took my bottom lip in and gently bit, only to chase away the sting with another glide of his tongue. I tightened my grip on him, tilted my head, closed my eyes, and deepened the kiss. The need to have his mouth fully on mine, his tongue tangling with mine and his taste mingling with mine was too much. I had to have it and right away.

When we pulled away, both breathless, I told him, "There's always going to be heartache in one way or another in life, but it's whether you can come out on the other side that matters. You did, Roman. I did too. We did it with good people at our back. Now you have me and I have you. We'll be there for each other."

"We will," he roughly stated. "Fuck," he clipped, right before he rolled to his back, bringing me with him to lay on him. When my hair fell around me, he stared up with heated eyes and cursed again. He thrust his hand into the back of my hair and brought me down to nip at my bottom lip. As soon as I gasped, his mouth moulded to mine, and his tongue slipped inside to tease me into a desire-fuelled frenzy.

My body reacted to his touch, his taste once more. I ground down on him, only to gasp again when I felt his hardness beneath me.

He tore his mouth away from mine, to curse, "Fuck, Nancy." His thumb ran over my lips slowly, I kissed the tip of it and then bit down, dragging another curse from him. "You undo me, darlin'. In all the right ways."

"So do you, Roman."

He grinned. "Yeah?"

"Oh, yes," I said, biting his thumb again. He moved fast. I let out a squeal when my back landed on the bed. He kissed me, his hand cupping my cheek, tilting my jaw up to deepen the kiss. I opened willingly for his tongue. His hips thrust into my side. Feeling his hardness again caused my heart to kick into the next speed. Excitement bubbled inside of me. It was me, an older woman, turning on a man twenty years younger, just from a touch.

Knowing it soaked my panties. I wished our jeans gone, but clothes magically disappearing couldn't actually happen. So I reached between us and pressed my hand on his jean-clad erection and gently squeezed. He groaned into my mouth. Hearing it, knowing how much he liked my touch caused my inner walls to clench. His lips trailed down my cheek to my neck, to my ear where he whispered, "You okay with me touchin' you?"

So damn sweet how he asked.

"Please."

He hummed under his breath and sucked my lobe into his mouth while I stroked him up and down. "Christ, darlin'. Your hand on me feels good," he said as his own slipped up my top. He tugged my bra down to free one breast and then lifted my tee enough so he could lean up and see me. His eyes hooded. He licked his lips and bent down to take my nipple into his mouth. I gripped harder around his cock, and he thrust faster.

"Tell me if you want to stop," he said before biting down on my nipple, swirling it with his tongue and then lathering kisses all over. My back arched. I knew I was panting, but I couldn't stop. My body was hyperaware of his touch, with the thrilling sensation it shot through my whole body.

Fingers trailed down my stomach, causing it to quiver. His chuckle was deep until my hand sank under his jeans and took hold of him skin to skin. "You feel good, Roman."

I ran my thumb over his tip, and he growled in the back of

his throat, returning his attention to my nipple. I lost his fingers dancing over my skin, but then his jeans loosened at the front and I knew he'd undone them. His fingers were quick to come back to me, to my jeans. He looked up at me, and our eyes clashed. He licked his way up slowly to my neck, just as slow as his fingers sinking into my jeans and beneath my panties.

His heated eyes stayed on mine, maybe to see if I didn't want his touch, but I did, so I smiled and spread my legs more. He groaned, "Beautiful," then kissed me just as his fingers slipped inside, bringing a moan from my lips.

"Roman," I breathed around his mouth, pushing down on his fingers.

He shifted back, looked down our bodies. "Fuck, Nancy. You look stunnin'." He pushed inside of me, in and out, and I knew my wetness coated him.

He pumped his cock into my hand. I'd been so lost on the feeling I'd paused. I gripped tighter, and he fucked himself in my hand while his fingers fucked me.

"Hell," he muttered against my neck, then kissed, sucked, nipped. His thumb pressed against my clit, and a cry escaped me. "Yeah, darlin'."

"Roman," I begged. "Close."

"I got you," he growled low. When his lips latched onto my nipple, I jutted down onto his fingers, and his thumb pressed against my clit with just the right pressure. I gasped. The swirling sensation in my lower stomach was stronger than it had been in such a long time. My eyes slammed closed from the thrill it drove into me, and then I came. Crying out, I threw my head into the pillow.

Roman kept at me until my body slowed its shaking. Once my breathing became steadier, I opened my eyes and smiled over at him. His grin was full of satisfaction. "You mind if I finish?" he asked.

I shook my head and started reaching for him again. His movement prevented me. He lay flat, pushed his jeans down, and took hold of his cock.

Despite being relaxed after my orgasm this brilliant man gave me, I perked up at the sight of my muscled man handling himself. When he stuck his wet fingers, the ones that had been inside of me, into his mouth and sucked, his hand on his cock jerked faster.

The sight was magnificent.

Rolling to my side, I shooed his hand away and took hold of him again. His eyes met mine. "Kiss me," he ordered. I did. He curled into me enough to slip his hand inside my jeans and panties again. I drew in a sharp breath as his fingers invaded me once more.

"Fuck, Nancy. Fuck, I'm gonna come." He shifted to his back again and his fingers slid out. "Want your juices around me when I do."

Holy Jesus.

I nodded. No words came to mind. My hands dropped away, and I watched him coat his cock in my cum. He pumped himself once, twice, on the third, his semen sprayed out the tip onto his tee. Another jerky hand movement and more spilled. Then again, and again.

Finally, he slowed, yet I wanted to watch that show all over again.

"That was…." I didn't have the right word.

He looked to me quickly. "Fuck, did you not like—"

My hand went over his mouth. "Don't question that in any way. It was the hottest moment I'd ever had, and I would like to do it again. Now."

His eyes flashed with heat. I dragged my hand from his mouth so I could snuggle into him, not caring about the mess, and kissed the man senseless.

He wrapped an arm around me and tugged me closer. His lips moved to my cheek, chin, neck, then back up to my temple.

"Glad you enjoyed that, darlin'. But we'll save the encore for another time soon." He rolled into me, glancing down between us with a smirk. "We'll both have to get changed before bed. Fuck, that's if you don't mind my sleepin' in here."

Shaking my head, I laughed. "You're crazy if you think of going anywhere after that. I like to spoon."

He chuckled. "I'm all for spoonin'." His face turned serious. "You okay?"

"Define okay? It you mean relaxed and turned on at the same time, happy and tired, then yes, I'm okay."

His smile was photograph-worthy and perfect enough to be sold to millions, but thankfully, it was only mine.

"Good."

"You okay?"

"If you mean exhausted after coming so hard I saw stars, and enjoying the state of my woman, then yeah, I'm okay."

Laughing, I nodded. "That's what I meant."

"Fuckin' thought so."

GAMER

Hugging her close, I kissed her temple. "You want a tee to sleep in?"

"I do have a bag with a nightie in it."

"Gonna get you a tee anyway. Like the thought of you in my clothes."

She bit her bottom lip, but I caught her pleased smile. It made me fucking feel good. I got out of bed, grabbed a tee, and dropped it beside her. Leaning in, I pressed my mouth to hers for a quick kiss. "Be back in a sec."

She nodded. I went into the en suite and cleaned up a bit, pulled on a new pair of boxers and a tee, then went back into the bedroom to see Nancy changed and back in bed. My dick jerked. Knew it'd be fucking unbelievably hot seeing her hair splayed out on my pillow.

Grinning like a fool, I stalked to the bed, jumped over her, which pulled a beautiful laugh from her, and slipped in beside her. "Let the snuggling begin."

She laughed again and scooted close. When she wrapped an arm around my waist, I put mine over her arm, and our legs entwined with each other's.

Perfect.

"Could stare at you all damn day long."

"Thank you."

I could see something was on her mind, the way she looked everywhere but at me. "What's up?"

"I'm not sure if this is the right time to talk about it."

"No matter if it's the right time or not, you can talk about anything whenever you want and I'll listen, darlin'."

"We're together," she said, and my gut twisted. Was she second-guessing us already?

"Yeah," I said cautiously.

"You're young."

I nodded, but she didn't see; her eyes were focussed on my chest. With my fingers, I tilted her head up until our gaze met. "Not too young."

"Thirty-seven, right?"

My lips twitched. "You been looking into me?"

She rolled her eyes. "Zara told me. How she knew I don't know. But... you know I'm fifty-five, yes?"

"Yeah, darlin'. What you gettin' at?"

"Kids," she whispered, looking away.

"Hey," I said, and her eyes came back. "After the upbringin' I had, I'm not wantin' kids. I just need a good woman and to have her in my bed and arms. Kids have never been on my cards or radar. If you'll let me, if things stay strong with us, which I hope to Christ they do, then I'm more than fuckin' happy to stand beside you with your family and help when I can."

Tears welled in her eyes. "I would like that a lot, Roman."

"Then that's what we'll have." I kissed her slowly. Her mouth deserved the attention, like all of her. "Now, we gonna sleep with nothin' worrying us?"

"Yes."

"Good night, darlin'."

"Night, Roman."

CHAPTER ELEVEN

GAMER

*A*fter two months of only seeing Nancy when I could get to Ballarat, I was officially over it. I hated not seeing her every damn day. While I managed to occasionally take her out for coffee or meet her for lunch at work—which her work colleagues gave her shit about, in a good way—it wasn't enough. We spoke all the time, sometimes multiple times a day, but her living an hour away from me killed. From that one single night of sleeping next to and waking up with her, beyond a doubt I wanted, hell, I fucking *needed* more. Seeing her every day would be a start. But I wanted to sleep next to her each night, not only to know she was safe, but having her in my arms was the only acceptable way forward. I just needed to figure out how to make that happen.

Things had picked up in all businesses that Hawks had a hand in, which meant more paperwork than ever before. Nancy was also taking extra shifts before the two weeks break she had planned.

Thank Christ that started next week. I'd also organised

with Dodge I'd be around less so I could head to Ballarat and stay in the compound there.

Shit a stick, that reminded me I hadn't spoken to Talon about it yet.

My phone on the deck rang. I was supposed to be on my way to Easton's for another barbeque, but I'd been delayed with a couple of things. Nancy was already headed my way, so I expected it to be her. Only it wasn't.

Dodge's name flashed over the screen. "Prez?"

"Get to Easton's. That cunt Andrew showed. East's got a few injuries, but he wanted me to call to tell you Nero's not good."

"What?" I clipped, already standing and making my way to the door.

"Long story short, Nero saved Easton, but got a bullet for it."

"Fuck," I barked, my gut churning with acid. "On my way."

The ride seemed to take longer than usual. I stormed through the house and spotted Easton sitting on the couch with a paramedic in front of him.

"I'm fine," he said. "Nero's in your room, resting on the bed."

Nodding, I strode down the hall and opened the door to the room I'd claimed when I'd stayed minding the dogs. Nero lay on the bed. He didn't even twitch when I entered. His gut had been bandaged, and he looked bad, goddamn bad. Seeing him like that made memories fly through my head and I gagged.

Whimpering.

Whining.

Barking.

Yelling.

A hand to the shoulder. Painfully tight grip. Forced to watch.

A choice to die myself or watch as he killed the animals I loved most.

Blood.

Tears.

Broken.

Dropping to my knees, I crawled over to the bed where Nero lay. My hand shook as I brought it up to his belly.

Breath.

He was alive.

He'd better stay that way.

Tears threatened, but I was a fucking biker and we didn't cry. I closed my eyes tightly and just took in his scent. I crowded him, my hands running over his body.

A door opened. My eyes sprung wide as I glared over my shoulder. My jaw clenched. "Nancy, go." I didn't want her to see me so fucking weak over an animal.

"No," she whispered.

"Nancy, fuckin' leave."

Nero whimpered in his sleep. I looked back down and shushed him, patted his head, his back. Nancy's warmth pressed against my back.

"Go," I bit out. Christ, I couldn't do this with her here; it wasn't right. She'd see me different—young, weak, and pathetic, all because of an animal.

"I won't," she said. "And if you tell me one more time to leave, Roman, I will kick you in the arse. You wanted me, you chose me, and I'm choosing you right back, no matter what happens. No matter if you think I won't like something about you, I will anyway because I know it's you trying to protect me from seeing something you think could change my mind about you. It won't, Roman."

I dropped my forehead to the mattress. "Fuck, Nancy."

She shifted around me, kneeling beside me. Her front covered my back as her arms curled around my waist. "He'll be okay."

"I know. God, I know, it was just…."

"Bringing up old memories."

Straightening, I twisted in her arms to land on my arse, and dragged her into my lap. "Yeah, it was." We sat for a few more moments in silence, just holding onto each other. It was what I needed. Damn, she was fucking perfect for me.

When I kissed her neck and gently nipped, she shuddered. "We'd better get back out there, but can you do me a favour?"

"Anything."

"Give me a moment?"

Her hand ran up and down my arm around her waist. "Of course. Since you asked nicely this time."

I chuckled. "Yeah, sorry for bein' a dick."

She smiled. "I understand why."

"Thanks for not listenin' to me and for threatenin' to kick my arse."

She kissed my shoulder. "Any time." As she stood, my hands slowly ran over her body. "I'll come back soon if you don't come out."

Winking, I tipped my chin to her. She walked out the door and closed it behind her.

She'd settled me. Calmed me.

Shifting, I leaned over Nero on the bed again, patting him. "Yeah, you'll be just fuckin' fine because you got East, Lan, Parker, not that anyone knows but me and Nancy, and then you got me."

95

NANCY

As I made my way out into the living area, I noticed Zara and Talon had arrived with the kids. There were quite a few others also, and since Zara and Talon were busy talking to Lan, I went over to Deanna and Griz, and told them I'd take the kids outside.

"When did you get here?" Deanna asked.

"Ah, just now." I didn't want anyone to head down the hall to disturb Roman. He needed his time.

"Nance, you takin' the kids out would be good," Griz said.

Nodding, I rounded the tribe up and herded them outside. Ruby and Drake ran off after the other dogs, who seemed just as excited to see them as they were. I'd started to close the door when I heard someone call, "Parker."

I glanced through the door in time to see Parker striding into the house, pushing the paramedic out of the way, and slamming his lips onto Easton's. I had my own little laugh at all the shocked expressions. I would have been one of them also if Roman hadn't said anything to me.

For a few moments, I sat there and watched the younger kids play. The older ones chatted, and I couldn't help but notice the way Maya looked at Texas. Ever since she broke up with her boyfriend a few weeks ago, because he was a dick and cheated on her—something Cody taught him a lesson about— I'd been certain she wouldn't take a chance on another boy so soon. It looked like Talon might have some trouble coming his way if he saw the way she was with Texas. At least he was a mini brother, with the plan to join Hawks when he was older. That could be a bad thing, I supposed, since Maya was a princess to the Hawks. It was what Talon and his men called her. Considering that, it could mean Texas wouldn't want anything to do with her. She imagined he'd think of her as off limits.

The back door opened suddenly. Talon and a couple of others stepped out and saw me sitting on the deck, alone and relaxed. Rolling my eyes, I turned back to the kids as everyone else filed out.

"Never expected that," Stoke commented.

"No one did," Talon replied.

"As long as they're happy," my girl said.

Talon curled his arm around Zara's shoulders. "Yeah, kitten. We don't give a fuck. Whatever floats their boat. Just a shock is all." Other brothers agreed in their own way—grunts or some type of noise and action in their macho way.

"I know." She smiled up at him. They were beautiful together. Their love showed in everything they did, the way they talked, teased, and touched.

Was it right to think Roman and I had that?

Only seeing him a handful of times over the last two months had been hard. Phone calls weren't enough. The brief day visits weren't enough. My chest ached when he wasn't close. Then when he was, I knew it wasn't going to be for long, and I couldn't really appreciate the time we had because he or I had to leave.

I missed his smile, his smirk, his laughter, his teasing, his gorgeous eyes that heated, warmed, and shone for me.

Would it be too soon to suggest a change?

Would he think I was crazy for looking for a nursing position in Caroline Springs?

We hadn't even had sex, and I was....

What was I?

Lost in him?

In lust with him?

Loved him?

Could I be?

I jumped when the back door opened again. I hadn't realised I'd been sitting there staring off in my own world, with my hand up resting against my heated cheek.

Thinking of Roman did that to me.

Turning, I spotted the man in my thoughts come through the door. He scanned the area and when his eyes landed on me, he grinned.

Good God, I had that.

He was mine.

He wanted to be mine.

I watched as he walked my way, saying greetings to whoever called out to him. The whole time his eyes stayed on me. His brows dipped at whatever he saw on my face. I wasn't even sure what it was myself.

Stopping in front of me, his hand came out. I took it, and he pulled me up, tucking me close to his front. "What's on your mind?"

"Gamer," I heard Talon clip.

Resting my hands on his chest, I met his gaze. "Nothing," I told him, because nothing was wrong. I just noticed I had what Zara had with Talon, what Deanna had with Griz, what Malinda had with Stoke.

How I got lucky to have it not once but twice in my life I didn't know.

I was grateful though.

So very grateful because the man in front of me loved me.

He hadn't said it, but I could see it, feel it.

He loved me.

And I loved him right back.

If it was too soon to make big decisions, I didn't care. I wouldn't go losing more time without Roman by my side. I wanted to come home to him, see him in the morning, just all the time really.

"Nancy, you're lookin' too serious. Darlin', what you thinkin'?"

I shook my head, smiling to hopefully reassure him. It wasn't the place to have a deep and meaningful conversation. That would come later, when I stayed the night.

My body shivered at the thought.

"Gamer," Talon warned, obviously not liking seeing me cosying up with Roman.

Roman growled under his breath. With a glare, he glanced over his shoulder and barked, "What?"

Talon scowled back. "You wanna step back." It wasn't a question.

Roman tensed. His arms fell away, and he turned to face Talon, tucking me behind him before he crossed his arms over his chest. Everyone around us had gone quiet.

"No, Talon, I don't wanna step back from my woman. You gotta accept this, brother. This is happenin'. Nancy's mine. I'm fuckin' hers. It's on its way to becoming a helluva lot more. When she's got her time off, I'm comin' to Ballarat to spend as much fuckin' time as I want with her because life just ain't the same when she ain't near. Said it before, brother. Prez. I'll say it again. Respect. You have it, but you keep not likin' what's happenin' with me and Nancy, then you'll lose it. If I have to, I'll leave Hawks—" Some of the women gasped. I gripped the back of Roman's cut.

"Roman," I begged, not wanting him to go too far.

"No need to threat, brother." Talon smirked. People relaxed

around us. "Hawks'll have your back. You just proved how serious you are with Nancy in front of everyone. I'll accept it now."

Roman's glare thawed a little. "Thank fuck for that."

"But if you fuck her over—"

"Jesus, you just can't help yourself." Roman shook his head. "Won't fuck her over ever. You also need to know I'll be comin' to you soon to ask to shift charters."

More gasps from women sounded, and I was one of them.

Roman's arm lifted and curled around my shoulders, bringing me close to his side and then to his front. He cupped my cheeks, staring down at my wide eyes.

"Was gonna talk to you tonight 'bout it."

"So was I," I admitted.

His head jerked back slightly. "Huh?"

Smiling, I told him, "I've been looking for positions in the hospital here."

He closed his eyes, but I caught how they melted softly, in warmth, in love. "Christ," he muttered. Opening his eyes, he asked, "You were gonna move here, leave your kids, grandkids, for me?"

I shrugged, acted like it was nothing where he knew, and so did I, it was a whole lot more than nothing. "Josie's here, and she'll have—"

"Nancy," he bit out.

Smiling softly, I nodded. "Yes. I was going to move here for you."

"Won't have it," he said before kissing me. I wanted to ask what he meant, but I got lost in his lips on mine.

CHAPTER TWELVE

GAMER

*a*fter Nancy saying she was already looking for a position in Caroline Springs, I wanted to drag her from Easton's place and show her how much her actions meant to me. Instead, after claiming her mouth in front of everyone, and a few kids yelling, "Eww," I pulled back and told her, "We'll talk later, yeah?"

"Um, yes?" Fuck, she looked good confused, turned on, and happy.

"Gonna be all good, darlin'."

"I believe you," she said.

No hesitation in her words. Christ, I was lucky she'd accepted me into her life.

Soon, Zara came over to capture her mum, no doubt to gossip. I spent my time talking shit with the brothers while watching my woman from afar. Watching her enjoying her time with her friends and family. Witnessing as she laughed, joked, and loved on everyone around her. She even shared a few heated looks with me, a secret smile of knowing where the night would lead.

At least, I fucking hoped she did. She'd said she'd stay, but did she realise it included me showing her how much she meant to me in ways our bodies connected? When a blush lit her cheeks, I could tell she was on the same page as I was.

Then when she licked her bottom lip and dragged it between her teeth, I'd had enough.

"Gonna head off," I told the brothers around me. Some chuckled, knowing, probably seeing the looks Nancy and I had shared. I didn't care. I caught Easton's eyes. "Keep me updated."

He nodded. "I will." I sent him a chin lift.

Making my way to Nancy, she saw my approach and stopped whatever she was saying to face me.

I stopped at her side, held my hand out. "You ready?"

"Yes." She smiled, taking my hand.

"Say goodbye," I told her.

"Bye," she said, not looking away from me.

Chuckling, I kissed her quickly, shouted a quick, "Later," to everyone and then walked out with my woman at my side.

Disappointment settled inside of me when I remembered we'd come in different vehicles so we'd have to travel to the compound separately.

"I'll follow you." She smiled as we stopped beside her car.

"How about I follow you?"

Her lips thinned. She shook her head. "No."

I snorted. "Why?"

"Because then I can't watch you on your bike. Preferably, your butt."

Laughter erupted out of me. I dragged her close and kissed her neck, still chuckling. "All right, darlin'. You wanna stare at your man's arse, you can. But drive safe."

"I will." She winked and climbed in.

I didn't want to look too eager, so instead of running,

which was what I wanted to do, I strode to my ride. Once on, I glanced behind me to find Nancy already staring at my arse. Chuckling, I kicked my girl to life and started off.

With Nancy's eyes on me, I grew hard. Usually, a ride would relax me, but I was amped up. I'd be in my woman for the first time very soon. And I knew she'd be willing to take me inside her also.

I pulled into the car park at the compound, and climbed off my ride. After taking off my helmet, I laid it on my seat and turned to see Nancy already walking my way with an overnight bag in her hand.

Fucking stunning.

"How was your drive?" I asked, smirking, taking the bag from her.

"Hot," she said, fanning herself.

Chuckling, I snaked my free arm around her shoulders and pulled her into me. "You know why we're here, right?"

"To play bingo?" she teased.

"Sure, we'll do that after."

"After what?"

I dipped my head. "After I get a better taste of that sweet pussy."

Her eyes closed, and a sound fell from her lips. She licked them as she opened her eyes, staring up at me with lust. "A-anything else?"

"Hmm, maybe."

"Like what?"

"Let's get in my room to find out."

"Sounds like a plan." With her hands on my waist, she shoved me back and started for the building. Grinning like a maniac, I watched her make her way to the door and stop there. She glanced behind her. Her brows dipped as she glanced around. When she saw me still near my bike, she quirked a brow. "Are you coming or am I doing this on my own?"

Smirking, I said, "I could watch while you do it on your own."

"Oh no, we're not doing that yet. I've waited long enough for you." She blushed, gazing around the empty car park. No one was about, maybe the prospects, but they'd be inside. Until I cleared them out.

Starting for her, I said, "You want your man?"

Her blush deepened, but she pulled her chin up and stated, "Yes."

Stopping in front of her, I grabbed the door handle and told her, "You'll get me then." I opened the door and kicked it the rest of the way. With a hand to her lower back, I ushered her in and down the hall.

Through the second door into the common area, I saw a few prospects tidying shit up, while a few club sluts hung around. "Out," I ordered.

Some startled, but all moved quickly towards the door. "Prospect, lock the door behind you."

"Yeah, brother."

Knowing he'd do as I'd said, I walked Nancy towards the hall where the bedrooms lay. She didn't seem to give a fuck they'd seen her with me or the fact they'd know what we'd be up to. If anything, Nancy squared her shoulders and strutted along with me.

Yeah, she was fucking made for me.

I opened my bedroom door and dumped Nancy's bag just inside it after she'd walked through.

"Still tidy," she commented with a cheeky smirk.

"Just for you," I told her. I wasn't really a slob, was taught to clean up after myself, but that wasn't a memory I wanted to ruin my night. Instead, I slid my hand to the back of her neck and tugged her into me. Her hands landed on my gut. She dragged them up my body. Her shiver told me she liked what she felt under my clothes. "You gonna kiss me, darlin'?"

"Yes," she whispered. Reaching up, she pulled my head down to meet her lips, and I fucking claimed them as I was supposed to. Like they were mine because they goddamn were.

I cupped her arse with my other hand and ground into her, showing her what she was doing to me. When her head dropped back, she moaned, and then she jumped. Not expecting it, I stumbled back a bit. Both of us laughed.

But then her face shuttered to serious.

"Nancy?"

She blinked up at me. "I know now isn't probably the best of time, but I want you to know I've only been with one other. I'm glad... no, I'm super ecstatic you've come into my life, Roman. That it's you I'll be with." She sucked in a deep breath and blurted the next part, "I've gone through menopause so I can't get pregnant, and I'd like you to come inside of me."

I stumbled again, nearly tumbling into her. My dick jerked behind my jeans, ready to do as she asked.

"Holy fuck, darlin'. You talk about me comin' in you there won't be any enjoyin' the night."

She grinned. "Then should we get the festivities started?"

"Fuck yes," I growled, and sucked her bottom lip between my teeth where I bit down. She moaned and rubbed herself against me. Never in my wildest dreams did I think Nancy would become a vixen in the bedroom.

I just hoped I'd be able to keep up with her.

Slowly releasing her legs, I let her slide down. I had to suck in a breath when nearly every inch rubbed against my stiff dick. Once she stood before me, I ripped my tee over my head and threw it to the floor.

My chest expanded when her eyes widened seeing me half-naked for the first time. Her mouth opened, closed, and opened again before snapping closed.

"Darlin'?"

"So big, firm." She poked my chest. I chuckled. "Tattoos, hard nipples, mountains of muscles." She glanced up to meet my amused eyes. "Can I take a photo and send it to Vanessa and Kari? They'll…. Nope, never mind. Only mine to see."

Christ, my chest expanded *again* at her words of possessiveness.

"Only for you, Nancy."

She clapped. "Yes."

Dropping my head back, I roared with laughter. When it waned, I opened my eyes and… "Fuckin' hell," I snarled. Nancy stood before me in her bra and panties. Her body rocked. It was fucking fine, but really no matter how it was, I'd still want her.

"You were taking too long."

I stepped closer, my arms going around her to unhook her bra.

Her hands cupped each breast over her bra to stop me taking it from her. I met her eyes, my brows rising in question. "I know this might ruin the moment, but… I have fears… I mean, I'm older than you, *way* older, so of course things change over time."

"Nancy." I growled out her name in warning. I didn't want her to talk shit about herself when I'd love all of her, no matter.

"No, wait. Um, you see, things change for a woman. My breasts aren't the same perky ones they used to be."

I fought off my smile and told her, "I've seen them before, darlin'."

She nodded. "Yes, you have. But I was lying down; it was different. They may have gone sideways a bit, but this is different."

"It won't be."

"It will be, Roman. Look, it's like… ah, they've gone to war and back. They've had a lot of stress over the years, with kids and such—"

Leaning in, I kissed her. She melted into me. Against her mouth, I said, "No matter what you think they look like, I'll fuckin' enjoy them because they're a part of you. You don't need to worry about my reaction, darlin'. Just lookin' at you gets me hard each and every damn time."

Straightening, I watched her suck in a breath and nod. She dropped her hands for me.

Slowly, I dragged her bra down her arms like I was unwrapping a present I knew I would love and wanted the anticipation to last. Fuck, finally having her two full handfuls in front of me was wank-worthy.

Shit, that sounded dickheadish.

Then again, maybe I should tell her, that way she'd know how bloody hot she still was. Or I could just show her.

Shaking my head, I leaned in while grinning. Nancy ran her tongue over her bottom lip. Her eyes widened a fraction as I kissed just above both nipples. My fucking heart kicked up its beat, my hips thrust forward on their own, and my cock throbbed.

Yeah, I wanted my woman something fierce.

Still, I took my time, lathering her breasts with kisses, licks, and then finally sucking her nipple into my mouth while I played and teased it with my tongue before moving onto the next. All the time, I looked at Nancy as she watched me enjoying her breast with a heated, wild look in her eyes. The whole time she gripped my shoulders tightly.

"Roman, please." She gasped as I bit down on her nipple. All worried thoughts left her and she was lost in feeling. Just what I wanted.

I hummed under my breath, enjoying her eagerness, but forcing myself to drag out her pleasure to drive her crazy just for me.

"You like my touch?"

She nodded. "Yes, very much."

I nibbled my way up her chest, her neck, to her ear. She shuddered. "You're fuckin' beautiful, Nancy. The way you look at me, every action and sound you make, what you say... fuckin' beautiful."

I kissed her neck, licked, and sucked hard. She moaned. "Y-you're mine."

Fuck yes.

"Yeah, darlin'. Yours," I said as our lips touched, and she opened under mine. I wrapped her tightly and dragged her forward, into me. Her arms closed around my neck. When she whimpered into my mouth, I ate it down.

Shifting one hand down, I tugged at her panties. Gasping, she pulled her mouth from mine. "Want them off?" she asked.

"Hell yes, darlin'. But let me. Then I want you spread on the bed. Your man's ready for dessert."

CHAPTER THIRTEEN

GAMER

*N*ancy gulped as I got on my knees before her. I gripped the side of her panties and gazed up. Her hand came up to run over my buzzcut and cheek. She nodded at me, and I hooked my fingers in the edges of her panties and ran them down her legs. My eyes landed on her trimmed pussy. Leaning in, I kissed her mound. She let out a small gasp that had my junk pulsing.

As soon as her panties were to her feet, she stepped out of them. I gave her mound another kiss, running my hands up the back of her legs to her hips, where I gripped and ordered, "Turn, show me that arse, and then get on the bed, darlin'."

"O-okay," she said shakily. She spun, and I palmed her arse cheeks, fucking kissed them too, then patted them. She moved to the bed, looked over her shoulder and smiled sweetly at me before she climbed on and rolled to her back, legs spread.

What a fucking sight. She was slick with need. I got to my feet, and she watched me as I undid my jeans and dragged them from my legs, along with my boxers. She gripped her tits and squeezed, eyeing my cock that jutted out towards her.

I walked to the bed, climbed between her legs and bent. "Hmm, darlin', I'm likin' very much what I see."

"G-good," she stuttered. Lust filled her eyes. Ducking in, I licked her from the bottom up to her clit where I sucked and tongued her. She cried out, forcing her pussy up higher into my mouth.

"You taste better than the sample I got last time." I kissed her thigh, her mound, and then made out with her pussy. She ground onto my face while playing with her tits.

"Roman," she uttered, as I paid special attention to her clit. "God, please. Need you inside of me." She didn't have to ask me twice. I could eat her out all day long, but if she wanted my cock, I'd give it to her.

Climbing up her body, I kissed her sweet like. She wasn't shy about tasting herself on my mouth. She moaned. I rubbed my dick against her entrance and told her, "Want your trust."

She nodded. "You have it."

"Want your passion."

"It's definitely there."

"Want your heart."

"It's now yours."

Christ yes. I slid inside of her slowly and watched her eyes close, her mouth open in a silent moan.

A grunted growl dropped from my lips when her walls tightened around me. Nancy stretched out, her legs went around my waist. Her eyes opened, and her hands slid out where she gripped the sheet beneath her.

"Fuck me, Roman."

My jaw clenched at her words. "You want me hard, darlin'?"

"Yes." Slowly, I withdrew from within her tight, drenched pussy and thrust back in hard. She gasped, nodding. "Yes, like that. Please."

I left one hand to the bed, the other I flattened over her stomach and dragged it up to cup her breast. I slammed into her. Another pleasant little gasp filled the room.

"Yes," she moaned. "More."

"You got it, darlin'." Pulling out, I glided my hand up and slid it around her neck. While I thrust deep, I applied pressure. Her eyes widened, but, fuck me, they darkened even more with desire.

My woman liked a little roughness.

Something I liked a hell of a lot.

"Yeah, Nancy," I encouraged while pushing in and out of her hotness.

"More," she gasped. I tightened my hand, and her whole body shivered. She was getting off on me choking her. Christ. Beauty.

Her hands glided to my forearms and then up. I swore with each hard thrust she got wetter. As her nails dug into my skin on my arms and dragged down, I threw my head back and groaned loudly, upping my thrusts. I released her neck, and she drew in a deep breath. Bending, I sucked her nipple into my mouth. Licking along skin so I could claim her lips, I then reached behind me. I grabbed her locked feet and shifted them. I parted them, and broke the fucking amazing kiss. She mewled in protest, but then I pulled out, and she glared.

Chuckling, I grabbed her hips. "Flip," I ordered.

Her glare disappeared. I watched, stroking my cock as her body moved and she got to her knees in front of me.

I slapped her arse and her legs came further apart, enough for me to get between them on my knees.

"Roman," Nancy panted. She wanted her man's cock back.

"Soon," I told her.

"Please," she begged, jutting her arse back my way. She

stilled when my fingers rubbed over her opening, down to her clit. I pinched, and she moaned so fucking loudly.

I eased my fingers back to her opening and dragged her juices up to her sexy arse, over her hole there. "One day, darlin'. This'll be mine."

She nodded, panting.

"You ever had it?'

"Never."

Fucking yes. Meant it was mine.

"Christ, darlin'. You're so fuckin' hot."

Lining up, I slammed my cock into her. She cried out, then moaned when I pulled out and did it again. I left one hand on her hip while I fucked her over and over, and moved the other hand up, into her goddamn fantastic hair.

Fisting it, I tugged her head back. She ground her cunt onto my cock and moaned low. "You like that?" I asked.

"Yes," she whispered. I twisted her hair more in my fist, and as I drilled into her wet pussy, I pulled her hair to a point where I was sure it'd hurt, yet all she did was moan, asking for more.

She was made for my type of fucking.

I pressed into her lower back with my palm, tugging her head back and to the side. My dick swelled inside of her from the look of ecstasy on her face. My tight grip ripped a moan from her lips.

"Roman, close."

"Fuck, darlin', me too."

"Yes. Harder."

I slammed into her over and over. Her pussy clenched around me when she was coming. My balls shot up. "Christ," growled. "So fuckin' good, darlin'."

"Yes, yes, you too." She panted. "Roman," she cried. A new pressure from her inner walls squeezed my cock tighter.

"Hell, fuck. Yes, Nancy. Come on me, darlin'."

She yelled through her climax. When I released her hair, she dropped forward and kept whimpering as her pussy kept coming. I grabbed her hips, held tight and snarled, "Comin', darlin'."

She hummed under her breath and then at the first shot inside of her, she looked over her shoulder and smiled.

Fucking hell. Perfect.

She wanted my jizz, she fucking got it.

With a slow thrust at the end, I gently pulled out of her and slid to lie beside her, bringing her close with me. Nancy curled into me, her arm across my waist, and her head on my chest. We were both still breathing hard, both spent after coming damn hard.

Licking my dry lips, I told Nancy, "This is how I'd like things to go. You tell me if you don't like any of it. We work, Nancy. You and me are it. You're mine, I'm yours. You have family in Ballarat. I would fuckin' never ask you to leave there. I'm gonna move to Ballarat, stay at the compound for a bit for you to get used to me bein' close. We'll take it how it's been, only addin' in more sleepovers."

She hummed. "That's a must."

I chuckled and held her tighter to me. Clearing my throat, I went for the next part. "Down the track or soon… whenever you're ready and only if you agree, I wanna buy a house in Ballarat for us. You pick. I don't care as long as you'll move in with me when the time comes." She stilled. "Know you love the house you're in, but, fuck, that's you and Richard's, darlin'. I don't wanna tarnish his memories for you and your kids in that house. It's just in me to have you in another house, another bed. Somethin' that's ours. If I'm being a dick for askin' that, and again I'm not talkin' about it being soon, then I'm sorry."

When she said nothing, my gut sank. I felt like punching myself for bringing it up right after what we just shared.

A sniffle caught my ears. I tensed, then rolled her to her back and hovered over her. She tried to duck away from me, but I cupped her cheek and brought her eyes up to mine. They were wet. "Ah, fuck, Nancy. I didn't mean—"

"Don't," she whispered, shaking her head. "These are happy tears, you doofus."

"Doofus?" I grinned.

"Yes." She nodded. Her arms came around my neck, and she brought me close. "Happy tears because you are the sweetest man thinking of not only me but my kids and grandkids."

I raised my brows. "Does this mean you'll seriously think about a house with me?"

"Yes, Roman, I will seriously think about a house with you." She lifted her head to kiss my lips and then dropped it back down, smiling up at me. "Though, I can honestly say it's a 99 percent chance I'll move in with you."

"Why's that 1 percent missing?"

"It's to see how good you are at cooking."

"Darlin', I'll blow your mind in the kitchen."

"I can think of other ways you can blow my mind."

"Yeah?"

"Yes. I saw a crosswords puzzle book on the way in. Let's see who can beat who at the answers."

"What do I get if I win?"

"Me. Naked. Ready for your ravishing."

Laughing, I shook my head. "Seems like I've already won."

Her smile grew. "It does, doesn't it." Her smile dropped a

little. "I do love you, Roman. I don't care if it's too soon. I want you to know."

My throat thickened. I cleared it. "Now I know I've definitely won in life with your love, Nancy. Fuckin' love you too, darlin'."

Her bottom lip trembled. "Kiss me."

"Always," I told her.

EPILOGUE

NANCY

*C*hristmas. Since Richard was gone, I dreaded waking up on Christmas Day knowing he wouldn't be there. Only the difference this year was the dream just before I woke.

Richard stood in front of me with a teasing smile. "Gamer?"

My bottom lip trembled. "Yes, I love him. Do you hate me?"

He reached out, running his hand slowly down my cheek to pinch my chin. "I could never hate you, Nance." He stepped closer. "You have a lot of love to give. Told you, you deserve that much and more in return."

"Richie Rich," I whispered. "You know I love you too?"

His smile was tender. "I know, and I'll love you forever and always. You would never do anything to take my love for you away. Enjoy your life, honey. Gamer is good for you."

Even in my dream it felt my heart was heavy. *"It's like you're leaving me again."*

"I'll always be around. I just wanted you to know you should never feel bad for anything you do. We'll see each other one day again, but not anytime soon." He leaned in and pressed his lips to my cheek, my temple, and then he bent to kiss just over my heart before,

116

with a cheeky smile, he straightened to kiss my lips. Dragging him against me, I wrapped my arms around him and held tightly. I wasn't ready for it to be over.

He pulled back enough to run his nose across mine. "Love you, my lady."

My bottom lip trembled, tears threatened. "Love you, always and forever, Richie Rich."

The dream had reassured me, though it wasn't like I needed it. I was too far gone in what I felt for Roman to ever go back. Glancing to the bed I'd just snuck out of, I watched Roman sleeping peacefully on his stomach, arm spread out my way. He'd been exhausting himself the last few months. Things hadn't gone to plan. He hadn't moved to Ballarat until recently, and that was after we'd bought a house together.

Everything was amazing. Brilliant even. More than I could ask for. There was something I felt Roman still needed in his life though.

Moving out of the bedroom, I walked down the hall and into the kitchen. The best part of the house was the fact it sat on land and it was close to Zara. But most of all, it had its own little flat at the back for when Josie and her men visited with my new grandbabies. I still couldn't believe she was going to have twins.

Just as I'd poured a coffee, there was a quiet knock on the front door. I glanced at the clock on the microwave and tightened my robe. He was right on time. Making my way into the living room, I headed to answer it.

Opening the door, I laughed when I saw Talon struggling with his handful. "Merry Christmas," I offered.

Talon glared. "Your present was up all night crying. Tell Roman I said good luck."

"I will." I smiled.

He handed me my bundle of mischief and turned, about to walk off, only to spin back around and quickly kiss my cheek. "Merry Christmas, Nancy. Good to see you happy." He straightened, saw the tears in my eyes and he grunted, "Better get back before the kids wake."

"I'll see you at lunch," I called. Talon waved over his shoulder, and I looked down to the monster sitting patiently in my arms. "He's a grumpy butt sometimes, but he's good for Zara." Moving back, I closed the door and spun around. "What are you doing awake?" I accused to a very still Roman, who had his arms crossed over his naked chest. I quickly glanced down. Damn, he'd put on black boxers. "Ah, he was supposed to be under the tree by the time you woke up, with a pretty little bow around his neck, but now you're not going to get that effect."

He didn't move or say anything.

"Um… Merry Christmas, handsome." I went for a smile.

Roman blinked. His eyes drifted down slowly to the French bulldog puppy in my hands, who let out a little whimper and started wriggling in my arms. Bending, I put him on the floor and right away he made a beeline for Roman.

Roman stared at the dog the whole way, right up to where it stopped in front of him and looked up.

"Roman, if I went too far—" My lips snapped shut when I saw the large shuddering breath Roman drew in. His arms dropped to his sides, his hands fisted, and I saw his eyes close tightly.

"Roman," I tried again, praying I hadn't pushed it too far. I knew how much dogs meant to him. I didn't want to hurt him, bring him unwanted memories from his past. I'd taken a chance that I was making the right choice on the gift. I wanted to bring him more joy into his life. Roman deserved it all, and I hoped a dog would be the perfect choice.

His eyes opened. The fierce emotions I saw in them caused me to suck in a breath. When his eyes snapped to me, they nearly rocked me back on my feet. They shone brighter than I'd ever seen, switching from warmth, to desire, to happiness as he stared at me.

He liked my gift.

No. Roman loved it.

Then he nodded, just before he knelt to the floor, picking up the puppy in his large arms and holding him close to his body. I was sure I heard a sniffle, but I ignored it because Roman being Roman, wouldn't want me to note it.

Instead, I made my way over to them. I knelt beside Roman, one hand at his back, the other patting the bulldog. "What will you name him?"

He shrugged. Clearing his throat, he sucked in another shuddering breath. "Merry Christmas, darlin'," he whispered, low and rough.

I kissed his shoulder. "Hope you like him."

Roman nodded. "Best fuckin' present anyone has ever given me, Nancy. The best." He pried his attention away from the happy puppy in his arms to smirk at me. "You've outdone my present."

"Well, really he's for both of us."

He shook his head, his eyes heating. "You got him thinkin' of me. Know you got him for me, really."

"I did," I admitted quietly. Roman leaned towards me, and I met his lips with mine. The kiss was slow and sweet.

He pulled back. "Thank you."

"You're welcome, but just so you know that when he cries of a night, you'll be getting up to tend him."

"At least I won't have to go far, he'll be in our room in his own bed."

"Roman—"

He kissed me, a quick peck. "In our room, darlin'."

"Okay," I whispered.

His hand snaked around me to grip my butt. "On the couch, darlin'. Gonna get your present."

Smiling, I popped up and walked quickly over, sitting with my hands clenched together on my lap. "Ready."

Roman chuckled. He stood with the dog in his arms and walked out of the room. He returned with a thin, wide box in his hand. "What do you think of Brooza for a name?"

"Brooza. Sounds perfect for him."

"Good," he said, handing me the box. He put Brooza on the floor and sat next to me on the couch. "You gonna open it or stare at it?"

"Um…." I was great at giving presents, never receiving them. I always worried I'd hate whatever I was given and it would show. I didn't want that to happen with Roman. I mean, I was the gift-giving queen. People always said my presents were the best. Would he feel disappointed over my reaction?

"Nancy."

"Open it," I stated and lifted the lid off. I placed that beside me on the floor, which Brooza pounced on, causing us both to laugh. When I removed the tissue paper, I stopped laughing and gasped. Tears immediately welled. My hands shook as I reached out and ran my fingers over the leather.

"Roman," I cried, completely rocked to the core with bliss over my gift.

"You my old lady?"

"Yes." I nodded. "Yes, very much yes."

"Then you got your own vest to tell everyone that."

Pulling it from the box, I gripped it to my chest. The bold words of *Gamer's Old Lady* touched me deeply, knowing he wanted to show everyone I was his. I already knew it, but having this, seeing it... God, it made me crazy with too many emotions to sort through.

The most important one though was love.

I loved the man at my side so damn much.

Facing him, I threw my arms around his shoulders and climbed onto his lap, still holding my vest. "I love it, love you. It's everything."

"Love you too, darlin'," he managed to say before I crashed my lips into his.

We would have our ups and downs, like any relationship, but I also knew we could get through any hurdle we had. Our together was the forever kind. And nothing was going to mess with us.

GAMER

Christ, my chest had just stopped aching with the amount of shit it felt when I saw her holding Brooza, and again when she'd told me he was for me. Then, when I saw the look on her face seeing my claim on her through the patch, it was like my chest expanded so goddamn far out to contain all the feelings and shit.

Nancy Alexander meant the world to me. She was everything. We'd never marry—I wouldn't do that to her kids—but I was fucking proud she was willing to at least wear my patch. I couldn't fucking wait to see what our future had in store for us.

Nancy leaned back after a few more lip touches to mine. "You make me so damn happy, Roman Power." If only she could know how much she made me feel. I didn't have enough words or actions for her to understand she was everything to me. "However, since you said Brooza was yours, I think you can clean that up."

It was then I smelt it.

"Fuck," I clipped, looking to the floor and seeing Brooza staring up at me with his shit all over him; he must have rolled in it. Laughing, Nancy climbed off my lap. "I'll get you a coffee."

"And you'll meet me in the shower."

Her eyes darkened. "And I'll meet you in the shower."

I watched her hips sway as she walked away. Once she was out of sight, I stared down at the little devil. If he wasn't so fucking cute, I'd be pissed as hell.

"You stink," I told him. He wagged his tail. Standing, I scooped him up and gagged. "Christ, you're lucky I'm gettin' some in the end."

Still, even with the dog shit, it was the best damn Christmas I'd ever had. Having dreamed of Nancy for years, I guessed they really did come true. Either that or she had just been out gamed by me.

ACKNOWLEDGEMENTS

I always struggled with this part, never knowing what to say and how to thank all the people who have helped me through this process. Still, I'll always go on because there's a group of people that help me in so many ways and I really appreciate it.

Becky, thank you for always pushing and being there for me when needed.

Lindsey and Amanda, thank you both for your help with Nancy and Gamer.

Wander and Andrey, you're both amazing!!

Letitia, the cover work is always wonderful, thank you.

Give Me Books Promotions, to all of the awesome ladies there, thank you for all of your help.

Leah Sharelle, you're one crazy but very loveable woman. Thank you for reaching out to me in the first place and I'm so glad you're in my life. There's no getting rid of me now.

To my nana, who will always be missed. I didn't expect to write a book using your name. I thought Nancy would just be a side character, but the readers have loved her, and I did want to bring her a happy ever after. I struggled a little writing your name in the sexy time parts, but Nancy shines through differently to what you were. She's just a little wilder.

To my readers, thank you for standing by my work. It brings me so much joy to know you want the Hawks to never end. As far as I have planned, they won't. In some way, the

Hawks will continue. I'd also like to thank you for reading not only the Hawks, but anything I write. That blind trust in my words means more to me than you know. You all rock!

My mum, sister Rachel, my husbutt Craig, my monsters Shayla and Jake, thank you for supporting me constantly.

ALSO BY LILA ROSE

Hawks MC: Ballarat Charter

Holding Out (FREE) Zara and Talon

Climbing Out: Griz and Deanna

Finding Out (novella) Killer and Ivy

Black Out: Blue and Clarinda

No Way Out: Stoke and Malinda

Coming Out (novella) Mattie and Julia

Hawks MC: Caroline Springs Charter

The Secret's Out: Pick, Billy and Josie

Hiding Out: Dodge and Willow

Down and Out: Dive and Mena

Living Without: Vicious and Nary

Walkout (novella) Dallas and Melissa

Hear Me Out: Beast and Knife

Breakout (novella) Handle and Della

Fallout: Fang and Poppy

Standalones related to the Hawks MC

Out of the Blue (Lan, Easton, and Parker's story)

Out Gamed (novella) (Nancy and Gamer's story)

Romantic comedies

Making Changes

Making Sense

Fumbled Love

Trinity Love Series

Left to Chance

Love of Liberty (novella)

Paranormal

Death (with Justine Littleton)

In The Dark